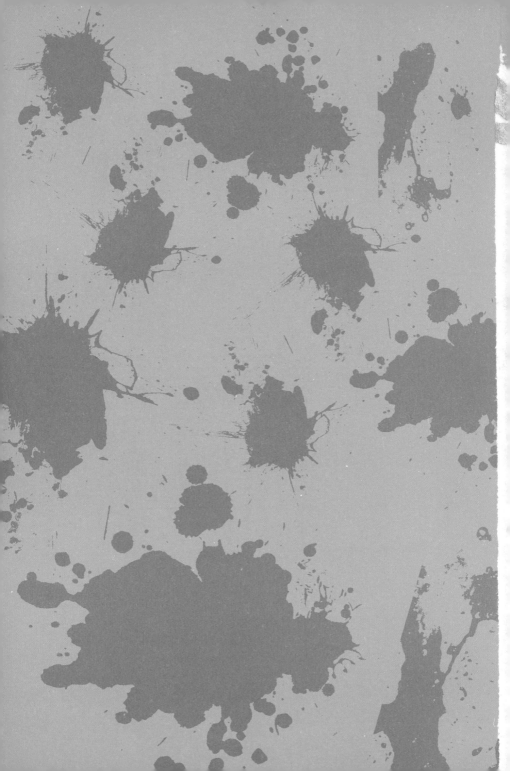

GARBAGE PAIL KIDS™

THRILLS AND CHILLS

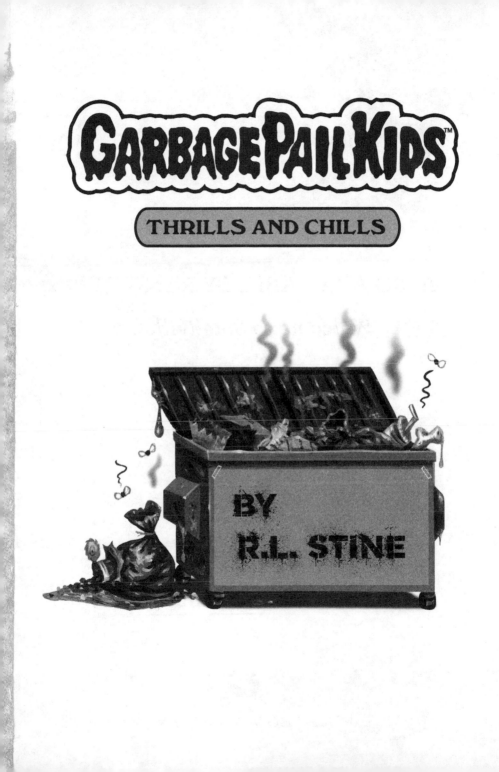

BY
R.L. STINE

ALSO AVAILABLE BY R.L. STINE

Welcome to Smellville

COMING SOON

Camp Daze

Illustrated by **JEFF ZAPATA**
Inks by **FRED WHEATON**

AMULET BOOKS • NEW YORK

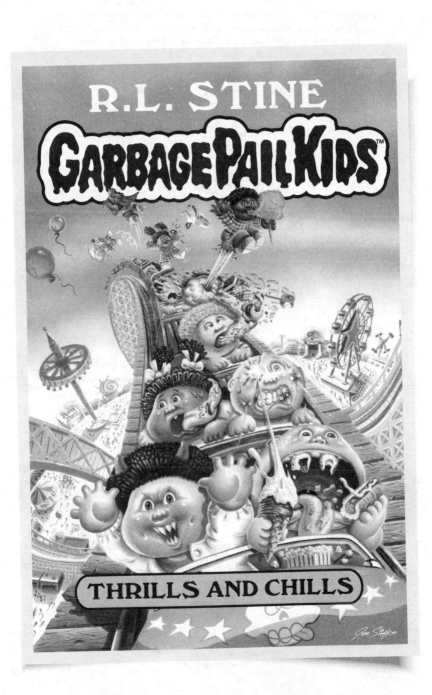

Cataloging-in-Publication Data has been applied for and may be obtained from the Library of Congress.

ISBN 978-1-4197-4363-4
B&N edition ISBN 978-1-4197-5800-3

By R.L. Stine
Interior illustrations by Jeff Zapata
Cover art by Joe Simko
Book design by Brenda E. Angelilli

Published in 2021 by Amulet Books, an imprint of ABRAMS. All rights reserved. No portion of this book may be reproduced, stored in a retrieval system, or transmitted in any form or by any means, mechanical, electronic, photocopying, recording, or otherwise, without written permission from the publisher.

Printed and bound in the United States
10 9 8 7 6 5 4 3 2 1

Amulet Books are available at special discounts when purchased in quantity for premiums and promotions as well as fundraising or educational use. Special editions can also be created to specification. For details, contact specialsales@abramsbooks.com or the address below.

Amulet Books® is a registered trademark of Harry N. Abrams, Inc.

ABRAMS The Art of Books
195 Broadway, New York, NY 10007
abramsbooks.com

"We're not
bad kids.
We just don't
know any
better."

Another dip into the garbage pail means another
thank-you to Ira Friedman of Topps and Charlie
Kochman of Abrams. They are not recyclable.
I need their expertise and knowledge at all times.

Meet the

ONE

Hi, my name is Adam Bomb, and welcome to Smellville. I thought I would introduce you to all my friends, but I'm about to **E-X-P-L-O-D-E** from shock.

I just returned home from my after-school Whack-a-Mole class (I take it for extra gym credit). But as I stepped into my living room, I nearly spit out my teeth when I saw my friend Rob Slob standing next to an enormous monster.

The room was dark, so it took a while for the creature to come into focus.

Rob Slob stood next to the beast and had one hand on its head. "Hey, Adam," Rob said. "This pig followed me home. Can I keep him?"

"Huh?" I made a loud choking sound, and my eyes almost popped out of my head, so I pushed them back in with two fingers.

"That's not a pig, Rob," I said. "It's a hippopotamus."

Rob scratched his hair. Whenever he does that, large insects fall to the floor. "That's weird," he murmured. "How did a hippopotamus follow me home?"

Brainy Janey walked into the room. Janey is a real brainiac. She's so smart, she reads books without pictures in them.

Janey stopped and studied the animal for a long minute. "I recognize it," she said finally. "It's a hippo from the *hippocrampulus* family. It's part of the river-wading family of reptiles."

See? Janey knows everything!

Rob scratched his head again, and a small toad hopped out from his hair. It bounced off the coffee table and scampered under the couch.

Rob probably should have a shampoo.

"Well, how did a hippo follow me home?" he asked.

"The Smellville Zoo ran out of money," Janey said. "They had to let their animals go."

The big gray hippo grunted, opened its jaws wide, and swallowed Rob's entire left arm.

Rob grinned. "Look . . . he likes me. Can I keep him? Can I keep him, please? He can stay in my room."

Janey and I helped Rob pull his arm free. "I don't

think he'll fit through the door," I said. "He's way too huge."

"No fat-shaming!" a voice cried. It was Babbling Brooke, and she came bursting into the room. "That's fat-shaming, Adam! Don't you know you're not allowed to make fun of overweight people anymore?"

I squeezed my fists at my sides and hoped I wouldn't explode. "You can't fat-shame a hippo, Brooke!" I cried. "Because that's what a hippo is—*huge!* It's as big as a . . . as a . . . *hippo!* Have you ever heard that expression before?"

Brooke bent down and slid her arms around the creature's neck. "He's sweet," she cooed. "If you ignore his looks and his breath."

The hippo nibbled on her fingers.

I saw that Pooper, our dog, had backed up to a far corner. Pooper eyed the hippo suspiciously, and the patchy fur on his back stood on end.

Behind me, Ptooey, our parrot, hopped up and down on his perch. **"How do you know?"** the parrot squawked. **"How do you know?"**

"How do we know *what?*" I asked.

"How do you know?" Ptooey repeated. **"How do you know? How do you know?"**

"How do we know WHAT?" I shouted.

"What!" the big parrot squawked. **"What! What! What!"**

Cranky Frankie wandered into the room. "Shut your yap!" he shouted at Ptooey.

"How do you know? How do you know? How do you know?"

Frankie made a disgusted face and sat down on the hippo's back. He probably thought we had moved the couch. "Who taught that bird to talk, anyway?" he mumbled.

"Who taught you to talk?" the parrot shot back.

"Shut your yap!" Frankie repeated. It's his favorite expression. "I found a new recipe for parrot chowder! Can't wait to try it."

"How do you know? How do you know? How do you know?"

"Frankie, you're sitting on a hippo," Babbling Brooke said.

Frankie sneered. "Yeah, sure. And you're standing on King Kong."

"No, seriously," Brooke said. "Look for yourself."

The hippo made a long, loud **BURRRP**. To be honest, I'm not sure what end of the hippo the sound came out of.

Frankie jumped up. "Shut your yap!" he shouted at the hippo.

Rob Slob rolled his eyes. "Frankie, don't you think it's surprising to see a hippo in the house?"

Frankie growled at Rob Slob. "I think it's surprising we let *you* in the house!"

"Where do hippos come from?" Babbling Brooke wondered out loud.

"They come from zoos," Brainy Janey answered. "That's their natural habitat. If you want to see a hippo in the wild, you have to go to a zoo."

"And what do they eat?" Brooke asked.

We all looked down. The hippo was gobbling up garbage that we had dropped on the living room rug.

Okay, okay. So we're not the neatest kids on the planet. Sometimes our garbage piles up.

"Look at him go with that garbage," Rob Slob said. "He's a total clean freak! He can be our new housekeeper!"

"Awesome idea!" I cried. "We won't even need a vacuum with this guy around."

I watched the hippo chew up a pair of shoes that were left in the corner. He really *was* cleaning up.

"So . . . I can keep him?" Rob Slob asked. "Can I?"

We all nodded yes.

"What are we going to name him?" Brooke asked.

Cranky Frankie snickered. "How about we call him Rob Slob Junior?"

And that was how Rob Slob Junior got his name.

We didn't have any more time to discuss it, because the front doorbell rang.

"That must be the hippo's owner coming to take him home," I said.

But I was very wrong.

TWO

I opened the door and found the Perfect twins, Peter and Patty, standing on our GO AWAY! doormat, with perfect smiles on their faces.

They wore matching red-and-blue polo shirts with the words I'M PERFECT on the front. And their white shorts looked like they had been starched and ironed, because they were smooth as steel.

Patty Perfect held a tan-and-white chihuahua in her hands. The dog had sparkly white teeth. It grinned at me with the same smile as the Perfect twins.

"You remember Good Boy," Patty asked, but it wasn't a question.

The dog stuck its paw out to shake hands.

I just stared at it and couldn't be more puzzled. What were Patty and Peter doing here? Whenever they saw

me or my friends, they always stuck their noses up at us as if we were garbage.

I squinted at the twins. "I can't believe you call your dog Good Boy."

"But that's his name," Peter said.

"I get that," I said. "But—"

"We named him Good Boy because he's so good," Patty said. She patted the little dog's head and he made a giggling sound.

"He's *perfect*," Peter said. "But we couldn't name him Perfect because our cat is named Mister Purrfect."

"Cute," Luke Puke said. And then he began to gag.

Junkfood John quickly stepped aside. He had a big bag of salted garlic prune twists in his hands. "What are you two doing here?" he asked the twins. "Are you selling Goody-Goody Scout cookies? Because I'll take six boxes."

I spun around to face him. "You already bought six boxes of Good-Goody Scout cookies," I reminded him.

He burped. "That was breakfast."

John's burp smelled of garlic and prunes. The Perfect twins staggered back and started to cough. Good Boy coughed, too.

When they finished coughing, Peter and Patty pushed past us into the living room. My other friends all jumped up from their chairs, surprised to see them.

Through the kitchen window, I could see Rob Slob Junior, our new hippo, helping himself to a garbage brunch in the backyard. Pooper, our big brown mutt, sniffed at Good Boy from across the room, then went back to sleep.

Patty and Peter walked to the kitchen and set their chihuahua down on our table. They frowned at the stacks of drippy, dirty dishes piled high. We don't always have time to wash them. We usually just eat our food out of the least dirty ones.

What's the harm?

"Did you come over to wash our dishes?" I asked.

They both shook their heads. "We can't wash dishes," Peter said. "The dishwashing soap is too harsh on our skin."

"We came over to show off Good Boy," Patty said. She patted the dog again, and I swear he went **HEE-HEE**.

Brainy Janey stepped up to the table. "I love chihuahuas," she said. "Did you know their name comes from the chihuahua plant? It means *friend* in Spanglish."

"I didn't know that," Peter said. "Are you sure?"

"Brainy Janey is always sure," I said. "She reads the kind of books you don't have to color."

"Chihuahuas are the result of two different breeds coming together," Janey continued. "The Chis and the Huahuas. In ancient times, the Huahuas were as big as elephants. So it's amazing the breed is so tiny today."

Peter pointed to the kitchen window. "Is that a Huahua in your backyard?"

"No, that's our new housekeeper," I said.

For a moment we all watched Rob Slob Junior snuffling up garbage from the lawn.

Patty rubbed Good Boy under his chin. "We came to show you the kinds of things Good Boy can do," she said.

"We're not trying to be show-offs," Peter said. "Because we're perfect. But we thought you should see this."

"Gather around, everyone," Patty said. "We want you to watch Good Boy."

THREE

Peter Perfect leaned over his dog. "Good Boy, stand on one hand."

Good Boy swung his skinny front paws down and kicked up with his rear paws. He arched his back and balanced carefully on his paw. Then he stayed there, his hind legs pointing straight up in the air.

"Now, cartwheel, Good Boy," Patty said.

The chihuahua did a perfect cartwheel, landing on his back paws.

"Backward cartwheel," Patty ordered.

The dog did a backward cartwheel, landing perfectly.

"I'm going to give the next command in French," Patty said, then turned to the dog. "*Chien, roulé, s'il vous plaît!*"

Good Boy rolled over.

"His French isn't as perfect as Peter's and mine," Patty said. "But he understands enough to obey instructions."

"Your dog is pretty good," I said. "But why are you showing us all these tricks?"

Peter raised a hand. "One more," he said. "You'll like this one."

He pulled a black handkerchief from his pocket and blindfolded the dog.

Patty placed a blank sheet of paper on the table in front of Good Boy. Then she stuck a black marker in the dog's paw.

"Okay, Good Boy, show us your ABCs," Peter said.

The chihuahua hunched over the paper and began to write the alphabet blindfolded. **A . . . B . . . C . . . D . . .**

"Are we supposed to be impressed?" Cranky Frankie asked. "His D looks like an O."

. . . E . . . F . . . G . . .

The dog filled the page with letters. When he finished, Peter Perfect pulled off the blindfold and petted the dog's head.

"Good boy, Good Boy!" Peter and Patty cheered together.

"He's a nice dog," I said. "But *why* did you bring him here?"

"Yeah. Why all the tricks?" Babbling Brooke demanded.

"Because we're entering Good Boy in the Smellville Pet Show," Patty said. "And Peter and I wanted you to see that you don't stand a chance."

"So don't waste your time," Peter said. "Don't even bother to enter your dog in the pet contest."

"Are you kidding me?" I cried. "Pooper is an awesome dog. He can win any contest. Pooper can . . . "

Patty glanced down at the living room rug. "Your dog isn't even housebroken," she said.

"Of *course* he isn't housebroken yet," I replied. "He's only four!"

The Perfects both tossed back their heads and laughed. They had tinkly, soft, perfect laughs.

"And one more thing," Peter said. "We'll tell you the awesome grand prize you're *not* going to win."

I sighed and felt my body getting ready to explode, but I held it in. "Okay, tell us," I said. "What's the awesome grand prize?"

"It's a free all-day trip to Six Thrills Amusement Park," Patty said. "But you can kiss that prize goodbye right now."

Their chihuahua stood up on his hind legs and threw kisses. **SMACK. SMACK.**

Wacky Jackie had been quiet the whole time. But

now she spoke up. "I *love* roller coasters!" she gushed. "Know my favorite? It's called the Stomach Punch."

"Huh? Why is it called the Stomach Punch?" Babbling Brooke asked.

"Because it takes your breath away," she said, flicking Brooke in the stomach with her fist.

Nervous Rex grabbed his belly. "Please don't talk about roller coasters," he groaned. "Roller coasters make me . . . nervous."

"*Walking* makes you nervous!" Cranky Frankie snapped.

"We have to go," Peter Perfect said, picking up Good Boy and tucking him under his arm.

"Mother and Father expect us home by five," Patty said. "Peter and I set the table for dinner. We also wash and dry the dishes *after* dinner. And do you know why? Because we're perfect."

"So? We don't wash our dishes," I told them. "What's the point? They only get dirty again."

As the Perfects started to the front door, Good Boy raised a paw and waved bye-bye. The door closed behind them.

I turned to the others. "We can't let the Perfects win another contest," I said. "What are we going to *do?*"

FOUR

Handy Sandy here. I'll tell the next part of the story, if you don't mind.

Adam Bomb started to pace back and forth, and he looked ready to explode. "We need a pet that can beat that show-off chihuahua," he said. "Anyone have any ideas?"

I had an idea, so I raised my hand. I'm the handiest kid in the house. I'm always inventing things and fixing things and coming up with the best ideas.

I don't want to brag, but I'm the one who invented the Virtual Flyswatter™ for killing flies online.

Everyone in our house loved that invention.

You might ask how the ten of us kids came to be living together in this big old house in Smellville.

And you may ask why we don't have any parents living with us.

And why we can't remember how we got here.

Well, you may ask those questions—but you won't get any answers. Because we don't have a clue.

Even Brainy Janey doesn't know. And Janey is so smart, she can spell her name backward and forward.

We only know there are ten of us in the house. And we have fun and take care of one another and don't fight—too much.

The other kids call us the Garbage Pail Kids, so that's what we call ourselves now, too. And it makes

sense, because our yard is jammed with garbage pails that are filled to the brim. We plan to empty them, just not right now.

But maybe our new housekeeper will.

Anyway, I raised my hand because I had a handy idea for solving our pet problem. "I could build us a *new pet*," I said.

The others all stared at me.

"I can build us our own perfect dog and insert artificial intelligence," I said. "I know I can build a winner."

Adam shook his head. "You already tried that. Remember, Sandy?"

"Well . . . yes," I admitted. "I built myself a little brother because I always wanted one. He was a great guy, too."

"And then his head fell off after a week. Remember, Sandy?" Cranky Frankie chimed in.

"I know, I know," I admitted. "He had a few flaws. But—"

Just then, Babbling Brooke jumped up from the couch. "Pooper can do it! I know he can win!" she cried. "I even made up a cheer for Pooper," Brooke said. "Here goes!"

Brooke wants to be a cheerleader so bad, and she's always making up cheers. She even tried to be a cheerleader for the debate team. But she never got picked for any cheerleading squad at school.

She jumped into the air, clapping her hands.

"GO, POOPER! GO, POOPER!

"YOU'RE SUPER!

"YOU'RE NOT A PARTY POOPER!

"YAAAAAY!"

"Ta-da!" Brooke landed hard and did a split on the floor. I think I heard some of her bones crack.

Pooper, our big hound, snored away in the corner. I don't think he appreciated Brooke's cheer.

Adam Bomb scratched his head. "I guess we have to give Pooper a chance," he said. "Maybe we can teach him some *new* tricks?"

"He only has *one* trick," Cranky Frankie said. "And we have to clean it up every time."

"Wake him," Adam said. "Let's see what he can do."

FIVE

Nervous Rex and Rob Slob crossed the room to wake Pooper up.

"How do we wake him?" Rex asked.

"Just poke him and say, *wake up*," Adam said.

Nervous Rex gasped. "I don't want to touch him. He has f-fleas."

"So do *you*!" said Cranky Frankie.

Rex started to shake. "What if he bites me?" he asked.

"Bite him back," Frankie said.

"I'll bite you!" Ptooey squawked, jumping up and down on his perch. **"Come over here, I'll bite you! I'll peck your teeth out!"**

"Shut your yap!" Cranky Frankie shouted at the parrot.

"Ptoooey! You shut your yap! Come over here and I'll peck your face into Swiss cheese!"

Junkfood John strolled in from the kitchen.

"Yummm." He had a glass jar in his hand. "These are awesome. Anyone want to try some salty raisins?"

"Those aren't raisins!" Wacky Jackie cried. "That's my bug collection!"

Junkfood John tossed a few more into his mouth and chewed for a while. "Hey—you're right. They *are* bugs!"

Rob Slob bent down and tried to lift Pooper's head off the floor, but the dog snored away. Rob grabbed the dog's floppy ears and pulled his head up.

Pooper didn't open his eyes.

Nervous Rex was trembling. "I th-think we should let him sleep."

"He's been sleeping since Tuesday," Wacky Jackie said. "Maybe he's dead."

Pooper snorted loudly but didn't open his eyes.

"He's not dead," Rex said. "If he was dead, he wouldn't smell this bad."

Rob Slob wrapped his arms around the big dog's middle and hoisted him onto his paws. The dog made a gulping sound and finally blinked his eyes open.

"Yaaaay!" Babbling Brooke cried. "We taught Pooper a new trick! Waking up!"

Wacky Jackie sat down on the floor beside Pooper. "Let me see if I can teach him some new tricks," she said. "I took a training course for dogs once."

I squinted at her. "You took a training course for dogs? Why? You're a human," I reminded her.

Jackie shrugged. "I wanted to see if I could pass it."

"How did you do?" I asked.

She sighed. "I got a C. I got nervous one day, and I bit the instructor."

Jackie turned to the dog. "Pooper—sit," she said.

The dog stared at her with his drippy brown eyes and didn't move.

"Sit, Pooper," she repeated.

The dog yawned.

"Don't start with a hard one like *sit*," Brooke said. "Try something easier."

"Pooper, stand up," Jackie instructed.

The dog sat down.

"Pooper, stand up," Jackie repeated.

Pooper yawned again.

"You're teaching him to yawn," Brooke said. "Maybe you can teach him to sneeze. The contest judges would love that."

"I'll try," Jackie said. She tickled Pooper's snout. "Sneeze, boy. Come on, sneeze."

Pooper yawned.

Adam Bomb shook his head. "Why do I have the feeling we are wasting our time?"

Pooper rolled over and went back to sleep. But before he did, he sneezed.

At least we think it was a sneeze.

Do sneezes smell?

SIX

Adam Bomb here again. Don't listen to Handy Sandy, I'll tell the story now. We all knew that Pooper was a loser. There was no way he would beat the Perfects' chihuahua in the pet show.

"We have no choice," I said. "We have to enter *Ptooey* in the contest." I turned to Brainy Janey. "What do you think of that idea?"

Janey shrugged. "I don't know," she said.

Everyone in the room gasped in shock.

Janey knows everything. Her brain is the size of a small planet. We've never heard the words "I don't know" come from her mouth.

"Maybe we could teach Ptooey to recite a poem," Handy Sandy said. "The judges would love that."

I turned again to Brainy Janey. "Think that's a good idea?"

She shrugged again. "Maybe," she murmured.

Oh, wow. Was Brainy Janey sick? Did she really say "maybe"?

"Let's see if Ptooey can learn a poem," Handy Sandy said.

Nervous Rex backed out of the room. "P-poems make me n-nervous," he said.

"Why do *poems* make you nervous?" I asked him.

He swallowed. "All those words. What if we don't know what they mean?"

"Awwwwk!" the parrot squawked. **"Come here! I've got a word for you! Ptooey!"**

I turned to Brainy Janey. "Do you know the best way to teach something new to a parrot?"

She blinked at me. "No . . . I don't."

I suddenly had a very bad feeling in the pit of my stomach. Janey wasn't acting all that *brainy*, and definitely not acting like *Janey*.

I stepped up to the perch. "Let's just try something out," I said.

We huddled around the parrot.

"Hey, his seed dish is empty!" Sandy said.

"Sorry," Junkfood John said. "I got a little hungry after breakfast."

"But you already had *two boxes* of toaster waffles after breakfast!" I said.

Junkfood John made a disgusted face. "They were kinda cold and hard."

"That's because you didn't toast them," I said.

He nodded. "You're probably right."

I poked Ptooey in the belly to get his attention and he snapped his beak at my finger.

"Missed. Listen to this, Ptooey," I said. "Let's see if you can recite a poem."

"**Awwwwk. I'll bite you! I'll bite you so hard!**"

I poked him again. "Just listen." I tried to remember a poem. "*I think that I shall never see, a poem lovely as a tree.*"

The parrot tilted his head to one side and stared at me with one round black eye.

"Go ahead. Repeat it," I said.

"**Awwwwk,**" the parrot squawked. "**Pete and Repeat were in a boat. Pete fell out. Who was left?**"

"Repeat," Wacky Jackie answered.

"**Awwwwk. Pete and Repeat were in a boat. Pete fell out. Who was left?**"

"Repeat," Wacky Jackie said.

"**Awwwwk. Pete and Repeat were in a boat. Pete fell out. Who was left?**"

"Repeat," Wacky Jackie said again.

"**Awwwwk. Pete and Repeat were in a boat. Pete fell out. Who was left?**"

I clapped my hand over Wacky Jackie's mouth. "Don't say it!" I shouted. "*Please*—don't say it!"

She pushed my hand away. "Don't say what? Repeat?"

"**Awwwwk. Pete and Repeat were in a boat. Pete fell out. Who was left?**"

"The bird is a loser," Cranky Frankie said. "Why tell such an old joke?"

"*Awwwk. You're* an old joke!" Ptooey squawked.

"I have a good recipe for linguini with parrot sauce," Frankie said.

I poked the bird in the belly again. "One more chance, Ptooey. I know you can do it. Repeat after me. *I think that I shall never see . . .*"

"*Awwwwk. Ptooey ptooey ptooey!*"

"*I think that I shall never see . . .* Come on, say it," I begged him.

"*Awwwk. Ptooey ptooey. I'll peck your nose hair!*"

"This isn't working," I said, sighing. "Our parrot is useless. The contest judges will hate him. *I* hate him."

"This is upsetting my stomach," Luke Puke said. "We need to get a new pet—fast!"

I turned to Brainy Janey. "Do you have any ideas?"

"Yes," she replied. "Yes, I do."

SEVEN

We all turned to Brainy Janey.

"What's your idea?" I asked.

She stared blankly at me. "I forget."

I squinted at her. "You *forgot* your idea?"

"It sort of slipped my mind," she said.

"Do you feel okay?"

"I think so," Janey said. "Oh, I remember my idea. I was thinking about a woodchuck."

"Huh?" My mouth dropped open. "A woodchuck? For a *pet*?"

Janey nodded.

"What's a woodchuck?" Wacky Jackie asked. "Is it some kind of animal made out of wood?"

"There's no such thing as a *woodchuck*," Babbling Brooke chimed in. "You're thinking of a *muskrat*."

Nervous Rex let out a **YELP**. "I'm terrified of

m-muskrats," he said in a trembling voice. "I've never heard of them. But I'm very afraid of them."

"There's no such thing as a *muskrat*," Junkfood John said. "You're thinking of a *hedgehog*."

"Hedgehogs are little pigs that live in hedges," Janey said. "At least, I think they are."

I reached out and placed my hand on Janey's forehead. It felt a little hot. "I think you may be sick," I said.

"Awwwk. You're sick!" Ptooey squawked. **"You make me sick! Awwwk!"**

Brainy Janey snapped her fingers. "How about a flea circus?" she said. "Rob Slob has fleas. We can pull them off him and train the fleas to do tricks."

I shook my head. "I don't think the judges would count fleas as pets."

"I also have dung beetles and dog ticks living in my hair," Rob Slob said. "Maybe *they'd* be good."

"Does the pet have to be alive?" Janey asked.

"I think you should go lie down," I said. "You're not thinking clearly, Janey. Your brain isn't working at all."

"Awwwk. You *sit* on your brain! Awwwwk."

"Somebody cover that bird," Cranky Frankie snapped.

"We need to call a doctor," Nervous Rex said. "All of a sudden, Janey's as dumb as we are!"

"I already called one," Handy Sandy said. "He'll be here in half an hour."

"Just enough time!" Wacky Jackie said.

"Enough time for what?" I asked her.

"Enough time to watch the new episode of *Jonny Pantsfalldown*," she replied.

Wacky Jackie and Junkfood John are obsessed with *Jonny Pantsfalldown*. It's a superhero TV show. There are about four hundred episodes—and they all end the exact same way.

I'm sure you can guess what happens to Jonny at the end.

But Jackie and John don't care. They've seen every

episode at least ten times. And yet they are always shocked and surprised by the ending!

They pulled Brainy Janey to the couch and clicked on the TV. "You can watch with us while we wait for the doctor," Jackie told her.

Uh-oh, I thought. *This might make Janey even dumber . . .*

JONNY PANTSFALLDOWN

Favorite TV superhero of Wacky Jackie and Junkfood John
Episode 455

Hold your breath, everyone! And keep your belt buckled tight for ADVENTURE! It's time for another thrilling episode of JONNY PANTSFALL-DOWN, told by me, the world's greatest sidekick— THE MIGHTY HAIRBALL!

"I will always protect you—unless I'm busy!"

That's what Jonny Pantsfalldown promised the good people of Pupick Falls. And he always keeps his word.

Every night, after a healthy dinner of jellyfish patties in larva juice, Jonny puts on his cape, his mask, and his Pants of Steel. Then, side by side with me—the Mighty Hairball—he fights crime and terrifies criminals with his famous battle cry:

YODEL-AY-EEE-OOOO!

Tonight, I found Jonny in his secret walk-in closet high above the cliffs of Pupick Falls. I grabbed a handkerchief and wiped the larva juice off his chin. It's one of the things a good sidekick does.

"We need to start cooking the jellyfish from now on," Jonny said. "They keep getting stuck in my teeth." Jonny has a booming deep voice, so loud it makes the wax in my ears ooze down the sides of my face.

He spit a jellyfish onto the floor. I quickly scooped it up with both hands and tucked it into my pocket.

A good sidekick—like me, the Mighty Hairball—is always ready to go into action.

Jonny was eager to get into his costume. But I saw that he was having trouble. He was tugging and squirming and groaning.

I knew what I had to do. After all, I graduated with a B-plus average from Sidekick School.

"Uh . . . Jonny," I said, stepping up to him. "The cape goes in the back, not the front."

He blinked at me. "Seriously?"

I wrapped my hands around the cape and tugged it to his back. "Better?"

"Much better," Jonny replied. "When I had the cape

in front, I kept tripping over it." He rubbed his nose. "The other night I fell right on my X-ray nose. And boy did it hurt."

He patted me on the shoulder with his new pair of perfumed, one-hundred-percent-imitation cotton gloves. "Hairball," he boomed. "Pupick Falls owes you a debt of gratitude." His voice was so loud, my nose began to bleed from both nostrils.

Jonny sat down and started to pull on his ultrasonic boots.

I wanted to be helpful again. "I think you have the left one and the right one mixed up."

Jonny shook his head. "It doesn't matter, Hairball. Both of my feet are right-handed."

He pulled the boots on and jumped to his feet. "Hairball, did you bring the steel suspenders I need to keep my pants up?"

I swallowed and blinked a few times. "No," I said. "Sorry, Jonny. I got busy weeding in the garden, and I completely forgot."

Jonny squinted at me. "Hairball, we don't have a garden," he boomed.

"Then why did I spend all that time in the dirt?" I demanded.

"Never mind, partner," Jonny replied. "We have to move into action. We have to find a crime. Crime won't wait for us."

He's very wise.

"Who is the criminal we are going to catch in the act tonight?" I asked.

"Big Bootus," Jonny answered. "We have to stop him. He plans to paint a naughty word on the side of the bank. And we have to get there before he can pull out his can of spray paint."

"Very good," I said. "But what if Big Bootus is wearing a disguise? How will we recognize him?"

"Easy," Jonny replied. "He has the biggest bootus in town."

Jonny swept his cape behind him and began to trot to the front door. Then he stopped—he likes to pause for dramatic effect. "Hairball, are you ready for action?" he demanded.

"Almost," I said. "I have one little problem."

"Problem? What problem?" Jonny asked.

"My head is stuck in the toilet."

JONNY PANTSFALLDOWN CONTINUED...

Jonny spun around.

I was standing right behind him with the toilet upside down over my head. I couldn't see him. But I could hear him.

"Hairball, how did you get the toilet bowl stuck on your head?" he boomed.

I didn't answer.

"Hairball—" Jonny shouted so loud the toilet rang like a bell. "Answer me. How did you get the toilet stuck on your head?"

"Please don't make me say it," I pleaded.

"You have no choice. A sidekick must answer every question," he said. "Remember, you took an oath."

"Okay, okay," I groaned. "I . . . thought it was my helmet."

"Your helmet is on the coffee table in the living room," Jonny said. "Remember? We were on the couch, eating cracker crumbs right from the box as a little snack?"

"Yes, I remember," I said. "My helmet and the toilet look a lot alike. Maybe I need to work on my sidekick costume. Jonny, can you help pull it off my head?"

"No problem," he answered. I felt him tugging at the toilet. Then I felt him tugging even harder. Then he stopped.

"What's wrong?" I asked. "Is it stuck too tight?"

"No," he said. "My pants fell down. It's because I don't have the steel suspenders to hold them up."

"Sorry," I murmured.

Jonny grabbed me hard by the shoulders and smashed my head into the wall. The porcelain toilet crumbled to pieces.

My head rang. "Jonny, I see stars!" I cried.

"Hairball, did you forget we have stars all over our wallpaper?"

I blinked, picking pieces of the toilet bowl out of my costume. He was right. The stars were on the wallpaper.

"No more time to lose. We have to hurry now," Jonny said, trotting to the door. "We can't let Big Bootus paint a naughty word on the bank wall. Not on *my* watch!"

Our secret headquarters stands on a high cliff, way above Pupick Falls. Jonny bent his knees, sprang up in the air—and started to fly toward town.

I get airsick, so I have to roll down the cliff.

It takes me a little longer to get there, and I get cut to pieces by the sharp rocks. But at least I'm not nauseous.

I caught up with Jonny at the edge of town. "We got here just in time," he said.

Just in time? I checked my watch. Then I remembered I left it on the coffee table.

"There he is," Jonny said, pointing with his imitation-cotton glove. "There's Big Bootus!"

I turned and saw him running full speed down the street. Yes, he did have the biggest bootus in town. And he was carrying a big can of spray paint as he ran.

"Stop right there!" Jonny boomed. "You won't be painting any naughty words tonight, Big Bootus! Not on *my* watch!"

Big Bootus tossed his head back and laughed. "Jonny, your deep voice may thrill a lot of people, including me. But I've come to paint! And I'll bet my big bootus you can't catch me in time!"

The race was on.

"**GRRRRR.**" Jonny let out an angry growl. Or maybe he had indigestion.

Then he shouted his famous battle cry. "**YODEL-AY-EEE-OOOO!**"

He lowered his shoulder like a football running back and took off after our criminal.

Big Bootus's boots thudded the street as he rocketed toward the bank.

He tossed his head back and laughed again. "I *live* to spray-paint naughty words!" he cried.

I watched them run down the middle of the street. "You're catching up, Jonny!" I shouted. "You're gonna get him!"

But then I saw Jonny's pants start to slip.

Jonny made a grab for them—but he was too late.

His Pants of Steel dropped down around his

knees. Then he tripped over them, staggered, and fell face down on the pavement. When Jonny sat up, he had tar stuck to his teeth. "If only I had those steel suspenders," he said with remorse.

We watched as Big Bootus ran up to the side of the bank. He raised his paint can and, giggling at the top of his voice, turned to us. "You lose!" he shouted. "Get ready for a totally naughty word!"

He pressed the nozzle of the spray paint can and aimed it at the wall. And in big, ragged letters he spelled out:

NERTS

I turned to Jonny and whispered, "Nerts? What's nerts?"

But Jonny was too angry and disappointed to hear me.

"I'll get you next time, Big Bootus!" he yelled through his sticky, tar-covered teeth. "Or my name isn't Jonny Pantsfalldown!"

That's our thrilling adventure for today, boys and girls. Until next time, this is the Mighty Hairball saying: "Keep your pants up—and reach for the stars!"

EIGHT

Hi, I'm Babbling Brooke. Back to our story.

We all sprawled around the living room as the exciting *Jonny Pantsfalldown* episode came to an end. Cranky Frankie shook his head. "I *knew* that would happen," he said. "I *knew* his pants would fall down."

"They fall down in *every* episode," Junkfood John told him.

"I've seen this episode ten times," Wacky Jackie said. "And his pants fall down every time."

"Maybe he should get smaller pants," Handy Sandy said.

"He can't," Jackie told her. "His pants are made of steel. They are one-size-fits-all."

"Guess what I did?" Junkfood John said. "I joined the Big Bootus Fan Club!"

"You've been in the Big Bootus club a long time!" Cranky Frankie joked.

Junkfood John looked confused. "What does he mean by that?"

Adam Bomb turned to Brainy Janey. "What do you think Jonny Pantsfalldown should do to solve his problem?" he asked her.

Janey shrugged. "Beats me."

A hush fell over the room. We all suddenly remembered we were waiting for the doctor to come and examine Janey.

Junkfood John raised the plastic bag he'd been munching from. "Anybody like to try this awesome new snack food?"

"What is it?" Wacky Jackie asked.

John checked the front of the bag. "They're called Cactus Needles," he said. "Very chewy."

He had needles sticking out from between his teeth. No one took him up on his offer.

"Hey, look what I found," I said, holding up my phone. "It's some kind of IQ test, I think. It's called 'Test Your Smarts.'"

"Janey, do you want to try it?" Adam Bomb asked.

Janey sighed. "It's probably too easy for me," she murmured.

"Let's see how you do," I said. I read question number one: "What is heavier? A one-ton bag of feathers or a two-ton bag of feathers?"

Janey rubbed her chin and thought about it. We all leaned forward, waiting for her to answer.

"I'm not sure," she said. "Can you go to the next question?"

I squinted at my phone and read the next question. "Which has more feathers—a duck or a plucked duck?"

Janey shook her head. "I pass," she said. "Next question."

"Okay," I said. "If a tuna swam three miles and a salmon swam five miles, how many miles did they swim altogether?"

Janey squinted up her face. "Were they really swimming together?" she asked.

We all groaned.

Something was definitely wrong with our brainiac friend.

"I know I'll get the next one," she said. "Brooke, ask me another question."

I read the next question: "If a train leaves the station at ten in the morning, what time is it?"

Janey rubbed her chin again. I could see she was thinking hard.

But the doorbell rang before she could answer.

Luckily, the doctor was here!

NINE

I opened the door and an older man in a plaid suit was standing there. He had wavy gray hair and a short beard and mustache. Behind his square-shaped eyeglasses, he had twinkly blue eyes.

He carried a black medical briefcase at his side—the kind you see in old movies.

"Did you call for a doctor?" he asked. He had a young voice for an older man. "I'm Dr. Nerse," he said.

"No, we didn't call for a nurse," I said.

"My nurse is away," he replied. "She's on vacation in the jungle."

"Why did she go to the jungle?" I asked.

"She has a pet monkey," he said, "and the monkey wanted to see where he grew up."

"Well . . . we need a doctor," I said.

He nodded his head. "I'm Dr. Nerse."

I rolled my eyes. "You'll have to make up your mind," I told him. "Are you a doctor or a nurse?"

"Yes, I am," he said.

Adam Bomb stepped up behind me. Adam studied the man in the doorway. "Brooke, what's taking so long?"

"He says he's Dr. Nurse," I said.

Adam squinted at the man. "Are you a doctor or a nurse?"

"Yes, I am," he replied again. He shifted his doctor bag from one hand to the other. "Do you have patients for me?"

"No, I don't have any patience," Adam said. "I'm pretty hot-headed. I don't have patience for much of anything. Sometimes, I totally explode."

"But do you have any patients in the house? Is there a sick person here?"

Adam nodded. "Yes. We need someone to check Brainy Janey. Her brain stopped working and we're very worried."

"Well, I'm Dr. Nerse," the man said. "Let's take a look at her."

He followed Adam and me into the living room and set down his black bag. "That's Janey," I said, pointing to her. She was sitting tensely in the big red armchair in the corner.

Dr. Nerse crossed the room to her. "Hello, Janey," he said. "I'm Dr. Nerse."

"I'm Janey," she said quietly.

"Awwwk. Ptooey!" the parrot chimed in from his perch. **"If you're a doctor, I'm a blue-nosed penguin!"**

The doctor ignored him. "What is Janey's problem?" he asked.

"It's her brain," Adam answered. "It stopped working."

"Well, let's take a look at you," Dr. Nerse said to Janey. "Do me a favor. Stick out your right hand."

Janey blinked. "My hand?"

"Yes," he replied. "Stick out your right hand."

Janey stuck out her right hand.

The doctor pulled a big wad of chewing gum from his mouth and pushed it into her palm. "Thanks," he said. "I needed to get rid of that. It lost its flavor."

"Can *I* have it?" Junkfood John asked.

Janey ignored him. But the doctor turned to look.

"It can't hurt to ask, right?" John said and shrugged.

The doctor ignored him. He opened his medical bag and pulled something from it. Then he turned back to Janey. "Open your mouth, please."

Janey squinted at him. "My mouth?"

He nodded. "Yes. Open wide."

Janey opened her mouth, and the doctor placed a cube of sugar onto her tongue.

Adam Bomb stepped up to Dr. Nerse. "Why did you do that?" he asked.

The doctor smiled. "Well, I usually work with horses, and sugar calms them down."

"Are you going to examine Janey's brain?" Adam asked.

"Yes, of course," he answered. "I Googled the brain before I came over here, so I know what I'm doing."

The doctor leaned toward Janey, but Junkfood John

stepped between them. "Doc, I need you to look at my mouth," he said. "It's hurting a lot!"

John opened his mouth wide and shoved his face up close to the doctor.

Dr. Nerse pulled down John's lower lip and gazed intently into John's mouth. "Hmmmmm," he murmured. "Hmmmm."

"Why does my mouth hurt?" John asked in a trembling voice.

"It looks like you've been eating cactus needles," Dr. Nerse said.

"Yes!" John cried. "Yes! That's it! This doctor is *awesome*! Brilliant!" He turned back to Dr. Nerse. "What is the cure?" he asked.

"Don't eat cactus needles."

"Brilliant!" John cried. "This man is a genius!"

"John, back off and let the doctor examine Janey," Adam Bomb said.

But Rob Slob moved in front of Dr. Nerse. "Doc, would you look at my feet? I don't know why, but I counted my toes this morning and I have fourteen."

The doctor let out a gasp. "You counted fourteen? Let me have a look." He bent down on his knees to examine Rob's bare feet.

Dr. Nerse gazed up at Rob. "Have you washed your feet lately?"

Rob nodded. "Yeah. I had a bath last year. Or . . . was it the year before?"

"Well . . ." The doctor frowned and shook his head. "You don't have fourteen toes. You only have ten toes. But you have worms living on your feet."

"Oh, thank goodness!" Rob Slob cried. "I thought I had a problem!"

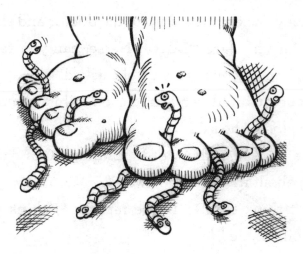

TEN

"Everyone stand back and let the doctor examine Janey," Adam Bomb said.

But Wacky Jackie pushed up to the doctor and shoved her arm into his face. "Doctor Nerse, can you tell me what this bump is on my arm?" she asked.

The doctor lifted her arm closer. "This bump? It's called an *elbow*," he said.

Jackie repeated the word. "El-bow? Can you do anything about it? Will it go away?"

"I don't think so," Dr. Nerse replied. "I think you'll have it your whole life."

Jackie sighed and shook her head. "My whole life," she muttered. "Wow."

Luke Puke had been sitting quietly in the corner. Now, he pushed Jackie aside and stuck his face up to the doctor's. "My name is Luke Puke," he announced.

"Can you tell me why I always feel like I have to vomit?"

Dr. Nerse thought for a while. "Perhaps it's your name," he said finally. "Did you ever think of changing it?"

Luke nodded. "Yeah. A while ago I thought of changing it to Barry Barf. But it didn't seem to help."

"Please step back, everyone," Adam Bomb pleaded. "I know you are all unwell, but Janey—"

"Just one more thing," I said. "Before the doctor examines Janey, I want to do a cheer for her."

"Brooke, please—" Adam started.

But I shoved him aside. "I've been practicing this cheer I made up for Janey, and I want to do it for her now," I said.

They all know I'm an awesome cheerleader, and I write amazing cheers. And I knew I could cheer Janey up before her exam.

So I jumped in the air, clapped my hands, and began my cheer.

"GO, JANEY! YOU'RE BRAINY!
"WHEN IT'S SUNNY, AND WHEN
**   IT'S RAINY!**
"DUH DO DO DUH DUH . . .
"DUH DUH DO DO DO!"

I did a perfect somersault and landed on my head. Then I staggered to my feet. It took a little while for the dizziness to go away. "Janey, did you love it?" I cried.

"What are all those *duh duh do do*s at the end?" Cranky Frankie asked.

"Well, I haven't finished it yet," I explained. "It takes time to write a good cheer."

I turned to Janey. "Did you like it?"

"Maybe," she said. She shrugged. "I'm not sure."

"I liked it," Dr. Nerse said. "It was very peppy. But do you always land on your head like that?"

"Usually," I said.

He frowned. "Maybe I'd better examine *your* brain!"

The doctor turned to Janey. She sat up straight and stiff. Her hands gripped the arms of the chair.

The doctor leaned close to her. "Do me a favor, Janey," he said. "Take several deep breaths and then blow the air out really hard."

Janey sucked in a deep breath and blew it out. Then another deep breath, which she blew out. Then another. She blew the air out of her mouth as hard as she could.

Dr. Nerse smiled and backed up a step.

"Why did you have Janey do that, Doctor?" I asked.

"It's hot in here," he said, "and I needed a little breeze."

"Awwwwk. Ptooey!" the parrot squawked from across the room. **"If he's a doctor, I'm a duck!"**

"Are you a real doctor?" Cranky Frankie asked.

"Of course I'm a doctor," Dr. Nerse replied. "If I wasn't a doctor, would I have a doctor bag?" He held up his black briefcase.

He moved behind Janey and pressed his hands against her temples. "Hmmm . . . your *mandingles* are firm," he said. "That's a good sign."

He stood up and rubbed the little gray beard on his chin. "I need to study Janey's brain," he said. "So I have to take a brain sample." He gazed around the room. "Does anyone have a teaspoon?"

ELEVEN

A teaspoon?

No one answered.

"A drinking straw will do, too," the doctor said. "I can go right up her nose and suck the brain sample down."

I gazed around the room. My friends were standing with their mouths hanging open, their eyes bulging. I think we all knew that we had a major problem with Dr. Nerse.

Before anyone could say anything, the floor started to shake. We heard thudding booms, like someone pounding a bass drum.

"Earthquake!" Dr. Nerse cried. "The house is shaking!"

I grabbed the side of the couch to keep from falling. Then I turned and realized it wasn't an earthquake. It was an enormous hippo thundering toward us.

Rob Slob Junior was back in the house.

We all screamed in surprise. Dr. Nerse shrieked in *horror*, and his beard practically flew off his face.

The big hippo didn't seem to like the doctor. Rob Slob Junior kept moving his enormous hippo jaws up and down as he charged. The hippo grabbed the doctor's bag and chewed it noisily.

Dr. Nerse screamed, "I'll send my bill in the morning!"

Then he took off, running. He burst out of the front door and scampered down the front lawn, with Rob Slob Junior galloping after him.

We all watched through the front window as our new housekeeper chewed a bite off the doctor's back bumper before his car could squeal away.

I heard laughter behind me. When I spun around, I saw Janey laughing her head off. She slapped the arms of the chair and laughed and laughed.

I ran over to her. "Janey, are you okay?" I said.

She wiped tears from her eyes. "That's just what I needed!" she exclaimed. "A good laugh!"

"You feel better?" Adam Bomb asked.

She nodded. "I feel fine. That hippo helped clear my head. I feel awesomely smart again."

Everyone cheered.

I saw that Nervous Rex was trembling. "What's the matter?" I asked him.

"Hippos make me n-nervous," he said.

"All animals bigger than a flea make you nervous," Cranky Frankie told him.

"Fleas make me nervous, too," Rex said. "What if a flea flies up my n-nose? What am I supposed to do about that?"

"We're not talking about fleas," Wacky Jackie said. "We're talking about hippos. Hippos won't fly up your nose."

"That hippo changed my life," Janey gushed. "I feel great now."

Handy Sandy squinted hard at Brainy Janey. "We have to test you," she said. "We have to make sure you're a brainiac again."

"Okay," Janey replied. "Ask me a question."

"Try this one," Sandy said. "Name the top seven mineral elements."

"No problem," said Janey. "There's iron . . . zinc . . . *calcimum . . . plotassliam . . . stodium . . . mangalese . . .* and pekinese."

"That sounds about right," I said. "Janey is definitely back."

We all cheered again.

"Okay, problem solved," Adam Bomb said, stepping to the center of the room. He gazed down at Pooper, who had slept through all the excitement.

"Now we have to talk about another problem," Adam said. "How are we going to win the Smellville Pet Show?"

TWELVE

Adam Bomb here again, continuing the story.

Junkfood John stepped in from the kitchen, wiping grease off his chin with the front of his T-shirt. He burped, and then his eyes bulged and he started to cough.

Sputtering and choking, he pulled a feather from his mouth. Then he coughed up another feather. And another.

I rushed over to him. "John, what's wrong?" I asked.

He spit out a few more feathers. "It's . . . it's the chicken I just ate," he stammered.

I rolled my eyes. "John, you're supposed to pull the feathers off *before* you cook the chicken," I said.

He shook his head. "I never remember that."

"What do the feathers taste like?" Babbling Brooke asked Junkfood John.

"They taste just like . . . chicken," he said.

Luke Puke let out a groan. "You actually ate *chicken feathers*? I feel sick." He covered his mouth with one hand and went running to the bathroom.

Brainy Janey climbed up from her chair. "Now that my brain is working again," she said, "I know *all* of the mineral elements. There's also nickel ... dime ... cobra ... aluminum ... *cockapoodle* ... geranium ... rice pudding ... mineral oil ..."

"That's enough!" I shouted. I could feel myself getting ready to explode. "Why won't anyone concentrate on our pet problem?"

"Yes, I agree," Nervous Rex chimed in. "All this talk about m-minerals makes me nervous."

"Get serious," Cranky Frankie snapped. "How can minerals make you nervous?"

Rex gritted his teeth. "What if I accidentally step on one?"

"Awwwwk. Ptooey!" the parrot cried from his perch. **"I'll step on *you*! Want to see parrot tracks on your skin? I'll step on your *face*! Awwwk."**

"Ptooey, shut your yap!" Cranky Frankie screamed.

"Awwk. You shut *your* yap!"

"You'd better shut up," Frankie warned. "I have a recipe for parrot à la mode."

"Ptooey. I have a recipe for Frankie Bite Your Face Off!"

"Why do we always have to argue?" Nervous Rex cried.

"Everyone just be quiet and think," I said. "We can't let Peter and Patty Perfect win another contest. We need to find a pet that will beat that chihuahua."

"It's impossible," Wacky Jackie whined. "The Perfects say their dog is a great ballroom dancer and speaks three different languages."

"Pooper is talented, too," Babbling Brooke said. "He can sit and roll over ... sometimes ... when he feels like it."

"Forget about Pooper," I said. "Sure, we love him, but he's a loser." I blinked and gazed at the rug. "Hey, whose turn was it to walk Pooper?"

Luke Puke raised his hand. "I think it was my turn."

"Well, you're too late," I said. "Now it's your turn to get a sponge and some paper towels and clean that up."

I opened the front windows to let out some of the smell.

"Does anyone have an idea about how we can beat the chihuahua?" I asked. "Anyone? Brainy Janey? Any ideas?"

"Well," she said, "there's *cobrium* ... malaria ... salt ... Saturn ... Uranus ... *plutomium* ... tinfoil ... *rubadub* ... copper ..."

"Hold on! Whoa! Wait a minute!" Handy Sandy jumped to her feet. "I think *I* have an idea!"

THIRTEEN

We all turned to Handy Sandy.

"Wait a minute," she said. "I'll be right back." She trotted out of the room and disappeared down the hall.

"Sandy is so handy," Wacky Jackie said. "She repaired my laptop *before* it was even broken."

"That's awesome," Babbling Brooke said. "She showed me how to use a screwdriver to floss my teeth. She's amazing!"

Sandy returned to the living room carrying a large rug. She held it up in front of her. "See this, guys? This is the white shag rug from my room."

We all gazed at it.

I shook my head. "Sandy, I don't think the judges will accept a shag rug as a pet."

"We could paint eyes on it!" Wacky Jackie suggested. "And a mouth."

"It won't work," I said.

"What if we gave it a tail?" Jackie asked.

Sandy frowned at us. "You don't get it. That's not my idea. I'm not suggesting my rug for a pet."

"Then what's your idea?" I said.

She waved the big furry rug in front of her. "The hippo! Let's say we wrap this rug around him and glue it on. He'll look like the hugest, furriest dog in history!"

"Brilliant!" Janey exclaimed. "I can see that I'm not the only brainiac in this house!"

"A furry Rob Slob Junior will make a great dog!" Rob Slob agreed. "How can he lose?"

I scratched my head. "How are we going to glue the rug to the hippo?" I asked.

"Easy," Sandy said. "I have something like two hundred tubes of Kwazy Glue in my room. I use it to keep my sneakers from sliding off my feet. It should be enough to give Rob Slob a nice furry coat."

"Hey!" Rob Slob said in protest.

"The hippo, not you."

"Oh. That's a relief."

"Yaaaay! We're gonna win! We're gonna win!" Everyone cheered and shouted.

66

Babbling Brooke moved to the center of the room and performed a cheer.

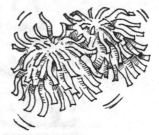

"GO, HIPPO ROB SLOB!
"YOU CAN DO THE JOB!
"GO, HIPPO, GO HIPPO,
"YOU WON'T SLIPPO!
"THE PERFECTS DON'T HAVE
    A CLUE
"BECAUSE WE'VE GOT ALL THE GLUE!
"YAAAAY!"

Brooke did a cartwheel, and her head slammed into the kitchen cabinet. The sound of shattering glass drowned out all the cheering in the room.

Could a shag rug hippo actually win the Smellville Pet Show?

I glanced out the front window and saw Rob Slob Junior chomping on our mailbox.

It was as good an idea as any. And the only one we had.

A SIMPLE WORKOUT EXERCISE FROM COACH SWETTYPANTS

Listen up, everyone!

I'm Coach Swettypants from Smellville Middle School.

If you've read thirteen chapters of this book, it means you've been SITTING TOO LONG.

So here's a simple workout exercise you can do to get the blood flowing, the heart pumping, and the muscles muscling. It doesn't take much time, and the only equipment you need is your body.

Shape up—or ship out! Don't just sit there waiting for Chapter Fourteen to start. Follow these simple instructions . . .

1. Put the book down and stand up.

2. Now pick up the book. How are you going to read my instructions if you put the book down?

3. Press your hands against your waist and push in—*push* until a little squeak escapes your mouth.

4. Press as hard as you can without screaming and stretch your back. Keep leaning backward till you hear a soft cracking sound.

5. Put your hands together and crack your knuckles loudly. This will help you forget the pain in your back.

6. Stand up as straight as you can and slowly bend your knees until you feel them pop.

7. Hold onto a chair and ease your knees back into their sockets.

8. Bring your head back as far as it will go and cry for help.

9. I've been doing this exercise along with you, and I seem to be in a lot of pain. I can't walk or move any of my body parts.

10. Can anyone help me? I'm in a lot of pain here.

11. I know you think this is supposed to be a funny book, but I'm serious. I need help right away.

12. Someone, please help me.

13. Is anyone out there? Anyone?

FOURTEEN

Hey, it's me, Nervous Rex. I get to tell the story from here. I sure hope I don't mess it up.

On the day of the pet show, I was so nervous I chewed all my fingernails *and* my toenails! I was breathing so hard, my chest went in and out like an accordion.

I kept thinking someone was at our front door—but it was just my knees knocking.

The Smellville Town Hall was packed with a huge crowd of people and pets. Adam Bomb, Handy Sandy, and I dragged Rob Slob Junior into the center ring. In his furry white rug, he looked amazing.

Our big problem had been trying to find a dog collar long enough to fit around his neck. The only thing we could find was one of Junkfood John's belts.

Adam Bomb and Handy Sandy kept tossing dog

biscuits into the hippo's open mouth. Sandy thought it might fool people into thinking he was a dog.

I gazed around the big arena. I saw Smellville town mayor Eli Crumbum on the far side of the hall. He was talking with Parker and Penny Perfect, the parents of the Perfect twins.

They were laughing and patting one another on the back. It looked like the contest was already over and Crumbum was congratulating them on winning.

I could feel my stomach sink to my knees. I was so nervous, I can't even describe how nervous I was. It felt like a big chicken was flapping its wings inside my chest.

My head was spinning. I sat down on Rob Slob Junior to help get myself together.

Just then, Patty and Peter Perfect walked up with big smiles on their faces. Patty cradled Good Boy, their chihuahua, in her arms.

"We are going around the arena and saying hi to all the losers," Patty said.

"That's because we're good sports," Peter added. He popped a little yellow tablet into Good Boy's mouth. "We feed him krill oil," he said. "It's good for his coat."

"Coat?" Adam Bomb cried. "Your dog doesn't have a coat!"

"Krill oil keeps his skin so smooth," Patty said, petting the little creature's head. "We drink it, too. It keeps our skin shiny and soft."

Peter Perfect glanced down at Rob Slob Junior "What do you feed *your dog*?" he asked.

"We feed him chihuahuas," Adam replied.

Good Boy uttered a **YELP**, and Peter and Patty took a step back.

Sandy dumped an entire box of dog biscuits into Rob Slob Junior's open mouth.

Patty Perfect frowned. "You might be overfeeding him," she said.

"He doesn't seem to mind," Adam replied.

Around the arena, contestants were lining up their pets. Dogs were barking. Two canaries in a wire cage were singing their hearts out, warming up their vocal cords. A white rat nibbled on a carrot stick as it ran furiously on a wheel.

I could feel myself getting more and more nervous. My eyes began rolling in my head. I couldn't control my face!

"That's a very large dog," Patty Perfect said. "What breed is he?"

"He's a cocker spaniel," Sandy said. "A cocker spaniel mix."

"Mixed with what? An elephant?" Peter Perfect joked.

The chihuahua went **HEE-HEE-HEE**. He liked the joke.

"Well, we'll see you after you lose the contest," Peter Perfect said. "And don't worry. We'll be very good sports about it. Because we're always perfect."

Good Boy stuck his tongue out at Rob Slob Junior and made a rude spitting noise. The Perfect twins turned and walked away.

Mayor Crumbum stepped up to a podium. His bald head was as round as a lollipop. And his eyes were so tiny, they looked like poppy seeds on a dinner roll.

He wore a long white shirt over white pants. That's because when he isn't busy being mayor, he drives an ice cream truck.

We always run after his Mr. Gooey ice cream truck because Mr. Gooey is the gooiest ice cream on earth. You just can't *believe* how gooey it is. It's awesome!

We all call him Mayor Gooey. But not when he can hear us.

"Welcome, everyone!" the mayor boomed into his microphone. "It's time for excitement. Let the Smellville Pet Show *begin!*"

FIFTEEN

"Have your pets ready!" Mayor Crumbum instructed. "I'll be coming down the row to judge each one."

Kids all pulled their pets into place, fluffing them up, making them stand straight and alert. I could feel the excitement in the room, and it made me very nervous. I sat on Rob Slob Junior's back, clasping my cold, clammy hands in my lap.

"Don't worry, contestants," Mayor Crumbum shouted. "Just because I love chihuahuas—and own eight of the delightful creatures myself—I will judge the pets fairly. I will not let my undying love for all chihuahuas stand in the way of my being a *fair* judge."

"Let's go home," Handy Sandy muttered to Adam Bomb. "There's no way we can win this."

Adam shook his head. "We're staying," he said. "Quitters never win and winners never lose and losers never quit."

Sandy squinted at Adam. "Are you losing it?"

It made perfect sense to me.

I rested on Rob Slob Junior's back as the mayor stepped up to the table to judge the Perfects' chihuahua.

Good Boy stuck out a paw, and the mayor shook hands with him. "Does he do any tricks?" Crumbum asked Peter and Patty.

"Watch this," Peter replied.

The dog reached a paw up to the mayor's ear—and pulled a quarter out of it.

Crumbum laughed. "That's a perfectly delightful magic trick. Why, how does he do that?"

Patty handed a deck of cards to the mayor. "Pick a card," she said. "Then put it back in the deck."

Crumbum pulled a card from the deck. He looked at it, then slid it back into the deck.

Patty placed the cards face down on the table. The audience in the arena grew silent as Good Boy began to go through the deck, using his snout to move the cards.

After a few tense moments, the chihuahua nosed a card from the deck.

Mayor Crumbum picked it up. "The four of hearts! Yes! That's my card!"

Applause rang out all around.

Peter Perfect fiddled with his phone. Music began to pour out.

A lot of people gasped as the chihuahua jumped onto his back toes and did a dance solo from *Swan Lake*.

When Good Boy finished and took a deep bow, Peter and Patty raised their dog high over their heads in victory.

The crowd cheered and shouted.

"*Bravo! Bravo!*"

"Come on, Adam. Let's go home," Handy Sandy said. "We're going to lose."

"Don't move," Adam said. "We're next. And I think we're gonna win."

SIXTEEN

I was so nervous I wrapped my arms around myself and hugged tightly until I could barely breathe. I turned away. I couldn't watch. I knew what would happen next.

"Good Boy has won our hearts!" Mayor Crumbum cried. "I have eight chihuahuas at home, but I can still be a fair judge. Now, I am sorry to say that we have just one more contestant—"

He gazed over at Rob Slob Junior.

"One more contestant for me to judge—before I award the grand prize to the Perfect family's amazing chihuahua superstar, Good Boy!"

More cheers rang out around the arena.

The Perfects raised their dog in the air again, and Good Boy took another bow.

The mayor stepped up to Rob Slob Junior. He gazed at the big creature, then made a face at Adam Bomb and Handy Sandy. "Where did you find this dog? In a swamp?"

"He's a special breed," Adam said.

Crumbum made another disgusted face. "Yuck. His fur looks like a shag rug. Pitiful."

Rob Slob Junior opened his jaws and let out a long burp.

"You need to teach your dog some manners," Crumbum said. "Please get this hippo of a dog out of here. I'm so sorry I had to see him. Now I'll never be able to *unsee* him."

"But don't you just love his adorable brown eyes?" Sandy asked.

Crumbum started to choke. "His eyes look like something I stepped in on the sidewalk!" he exclaimed.

"Does that mean we don't win?" Adam asked.

Crumbum sputtered and his face turned bright red. "You're lucky I don't have you arrested!" he cried.

"Arrested? For what?" Adam asked.

"I'll think of something!" the mayor snapped.

"You're hurting our dog's feelings," Sandy told the mayor.

"Please step aside," Crumbum begged. He raised a big blue ribbon. "It's time for me to award the grand prize to that amazing chihuahua. The perfectly perfect Good Boy."

Before the mayor could turn around, Rob Slob Junior decided to move. He lowered his broad head and shook his fur-covered body. Then he took four heavy steps forward.

I turned just in time to see our hippo open his mouth wide—and swallow the Perfects' chihuahua whole.

SEVENTEEN

Gasps and loud cries of horror echoed across the big arena.

I shut my eyes and held my breath. I'd never been so nervous in my life.

If Good Boy was eaten, the mayor would have no choice. He would have to name Rob Slob Junior the winner.

Was it possible? I crossed all my fingers *and* my toes.

The mayor's mouth dropped open and his tiny eyes almost popped off his round head. He dropped the blue ribbon to the floor. "Nooooooo!" he howled.

Peter Perfect let out a moan and passed out in Patty Perfect's arms.

The mayor grabbed the sides of Rob Slob Junior's big head and shouted at Adam and Sandy. "Make him open his mouth! Make your dog open his mouth!"

"How?" Adam cried. "We don't know how to do that."

"Didn't you train your dog?" Crumbum shouted.

"Not all that much," Adam said.

I stared at the hippo. His jaws were clamped tightly shut.

"Let me try something," Handy Sandy said.

She squatted down beside the hippo. Then she reached out and tickled him under his huge chin.

"Tickle tickle tickle."

We all watched. Everyone in the Town Hall arena watched. No one made a sound. No one breathed.

"Tickle tickle tickle."

Rob Slob Junior uttered a soft giggle, and his mouth swung open.

I saw Good Boy sitting on the hippo's wide pink tongue. He was very shiny, all covered in slobber.

When Rob Slob Junior's mouth opened wide, the chihuahua bolted forward. Good Boy leaped out of the hippo's mouth—and took off!

Patty Perfect cried out in alarm. "Wait! Good Boy— wait!" she shouted. "Stop! Stop running!"

Peter opened his eyes and called out *"Arrête de courir!"* in French, in case the frightened dog had forgotten his English.

But the little chihuahua wouldn't stop. He ran across the arena, through the crowd, up the stairs, and out the door. In thirty seconds he was gone. Vanished.

The Perfect twins sighed and collapsed to their knees.

"He's pretty fast for a chihuahua," Handy Sandy said.

"So that's *our* magic trick," Adam Bomb explained. "Rob Slob Junior made Good Boy disappear. Then he brought him back. Oh, and made him disappear again. That's *three* tricks in one!"

The mayor stood there red-faced, gritting his teeth,

squeezing his hands into fists, trembling with anger. Finally, he picked up the blue-ribbon award from the floor.

"I hate to do this," he said, turning to Adam, Sandy, and me. "I really really really really really hate to do this. I would much rather smash in my own head with a sledgehammer. But . . ."

But?

The three of us waited in silence for him to finish.

"But I am going to award the grand prize to you and your hideous animal."

"*Wait!*" a voice shouted.

"*Wait! Please Wait!*"

"Huh?" I gasped. I turned to see five kids running toward us across the center of the arena. One of them carried a big black cat!

"Oh, wow!" I cried as they ran closer. "Look at them!"

Adam Bomb slapped his forehead. His eyes bulged out of his head. "Look at them! Look at them!" he screamed. "I . . . I don't *believe* it!"

EIGHTEEN

Adam Bomb here. I have to continue telling you the *shocking* part of this story. Rex was too nervous, and had his eyes closed for most of this.

And it *was* shocking. I stared in amazement at the five kids carrying their black cat into the arena. We all stared, shaking our heads, mumbling and muttering, and nearly choking with surprise.

As we stared, our other friends—the kids from our house—came rocketing down from their seats to join us. Now all *ten* of us were staring in shock and amazement and disbelief and anything else you can think to call it.

My head was spinning. My chest was tightening. I held my breath to keep from totally *exploding*!

The five of them stopped running when they saw us.

"HUH?"

"WHA—?"

"WHYA—?"
"WHOA!"
"AAACK."

They gasped and groaned and muttered and moaned just like us. The five of them stared at the ten of us. It was the longest staring match I've ever been in.

Why?

Why were we all so shocked and amazed?

I'll tell you why. It was because the five of them *looked just like us!*

I mean, we Garbage Pail Kids *know* we're not normal. The Perfect twins are the *normal* kids. And we are *nothing* like the Perfect twins or any of the other kids at Smellville Middle School.

We know we're different. We're different and we're proud. (Most of the time.)

But now we were standing in the middle of the arena, staring at five kids who also looked . . . *different.*

The arena grew silent as we all stared at one another.

Finally, Cranky Frankie broke the silence. "Who *are* you?" he asked.

"Yeah, what are your names?" Wacky Jackie demanded.

They went down the line.

"I'm Windy Winston."

"I'm Nat Nerd."

"I'm Brett Sweat."

"I'm Nasty Nancy. Want to make something of it?"

The last kid had been picking his nose the whole time. He pulled his finger out and wiped it on his jeans. "And I'm Disgustin' Justin," he said.

"This can't be happening," I muttered. "Are they for real? Or did they come here to make fun of us?"

The kid named Windy Winston took a few steps toward us. "We call ourselves the Garbage Pail Kids," he said.

"No way!" Cranky Frankie shouted.

"That's a lie," I cried. *"We're* the Garbage Pail Kids!"

"No, you're not!"

"Yes, we are!"

"No, you're not!"

"You look like *garbage,*" Nasty Nancy said. "But *we're* the Garbage Pail Kids."

"Fakes!"

"You're the fakes!"

"You're fake garbage!"

"You smell like garbage!"

It was starting to get nasty. My head started to

throb. My heart was thudding like a jackhammer in my chest.

"Whoa. Hold on," Brainy Janey chimed in. "Why do the five of you call yourselves the Garbage Pail Kids?"

"I'll tell you why," Disgustin' Justin replied. "Because we live behind a bunch of garbage pails."

"No way!" I cried. *"We* live behind garbage pails. *We* do—not you!"

"We do! You're a bunch of fakes! Fake garbage!"

"You're the fakers! You are!"

"I know *we're* garbage, but what are *you*?"

This was too weird. Too shocking. Too unbelievable.

Everyone was shouting and pointing fingers.

I couldn't take any more. My head throbbed harder. My chest pulsed and throbbed.

I told you my name is Adam Bomb. And you know what happens to me . . . **BAAAAAAAAAAAAAAA-RRRRRRRRRRRROOOOOOOOMMMMMM!**

First, my head EXPLODED—and then my whole body!

What a mess. What a horrible mess.

And all over the floor of Smellville Town Hall, too.

Meet the NEW

NINETEEN

Brainy Janey here. I have to continue the story since Adam Bomb exploded all over the place. Cranky Frankie and Junkfood John carried him away. But don't worry. He'll be fine. He just does that from time to time. It's kinda his thing.

Once the others got over the shock, we all started to fight and shout and point again. But Mayor Crumbum stepped between us and broke things up.

"Shut up! Everyone shut up!" he shouted, waving his hands above his head. "Shut up—or I'll award the grand prize to that chihuahua, even though he ran away."

"Yaaaay." Peter and Patty Perfect clapped.

"You two shut up, too," the mayor snapped.

The Perfects gasped.

Brett Sweat wiped sweat off his face with the front of his T-shirt. "What *is* the grand prize, anyway?"

"The grand prize," Crumbum answered, "is a free all-day trip to Six Thrills Amusement Park!"

"You're joking," Nasty Nancy said. "I went to Six Thrills once and I only had *five* thrills!"

"Don't worry about it," Junkfood John told her. "You're not going to win anyway. Your cat can't beat our . . . uh . . . dog."

I gazed down at our furry pet. Rob Slob Junior was chewing on one of Luke Puke's sneakers. Luke didn't look happy.

"Our cat is named Winner," Windy Winston said. "That's because he's going to *win* the contest."

"Winner is a *loser*," Wacky Jackie snapped.

"Stand back, everyone," Mayor Crumbum ordered. "Back. Get back. Let's see what this *cat* can do. I'm allergic to cats, but I can still be a fair judge."

Brett Sweat wiped his face on the front of Mayor Crumbum's shirt. Then he placed the big cat on a stool.

Nat Nerd handed the cat a violin and bow.

We all stood around watching in silence as the cat sat up and tapped one back paw on the table to set the

rhythm. Then the cat pulled the bow over the violin—
and played a complete violin concerto by Mendelssohn.

When the cat finished, the auditorium remained
silent. The audience had tears in their eyes. The music
was so beautiful, some people were sobbing. Others
held the person next to them and hugged.

Mayor Crumbum wiped tears off his cheeks. He
raised the blue ribbon above the black cat's head. "I
think Winner is the winner!" he exclaimed.

TWENTY

"Not fair!" cried Patty Perfect. "Not fair at all!"

"Good Boy plays that concerto in his sleep!" Peter Perfect exclaimed. "Just last week, he *burped* the whole concerto! And it didn't smell one bit, either."

"Your dog ran away," Babbling Brooke shouted. "Your dog is a quitter!"

"He's not a quitter!" Patty protested. "He just got shook up because your dog tried to *eat* him!"

"Rob Slob Junior didn't try to eat him," I explained. "He simply gave your dog a big kiss."

"You call that a kiss?" Peter cried. "If that was a kiss, your dog has some pretty big lips!"

"No fat-shaming!" Babbling Brooke cried.

"Stop fighting!" Nasty Nancy shouted. "Our cat won fair and square."

Disgustin' Justin shoved Junkfood John with both hands. "You're all a bunch of bad sports!" he yelled.

"*You're* the bad sports!" Babbling Brooke cried. "You came too late to enter the contest! You can't just show up at the last minute."

The argument turned into a shoving match, with everyone shoving everyone else.

Even people in the audience started to shove one another, taking one side over the others.

"*Good Boy!*"

"*Rob Slob Junior!*"

"*Winner!*"

Nervous Rex backed away and hugged himself. His legs were trembling so hard, it looked like he was dancing.

Junkfood John had a big bag of tortilla chips tilted into his mouth. He always eats when he's nervous. (And when he's not nervous.)

The girl called Nasty Nancy was so worked up, she started to *punch herself!*

Mayor Crumbum ducked under a table, his hands over his ears. "Break it up! Break it up, guys!" he kept shouting.

Nat Nerd leaped up onto the table. He cupped his

hands around his mouth and cried at the top of his lungs: "Manners, everyone! Remember your manners!"

The auditorium fell silent. The shoving stopped.

Then there was a loud *crunch*. I looked down and saw our hippo gobbling up the black cat's violin.

The mayor climbed out from under the table. "The boy standing on the table is right. Everyone—manners! Stop and calm down," he said. *"No more shoving. Or yelling!"*

"We'll stop after we *win*!" Cranky Frankie cried.

"Enough," Crumbum said. "I declare this contest a *tie*! You *all* win. You all win a trip to Six Thrills Amusement Park!"

Everyone cheered. Babbling Brooke jumped up and down and then did a cartwheel.

"YAAAAAY!"

The sound echoed off the arena walls.

"A TIE! A TIE!"

"No way!" Crankie Frankie shouted over the cheers. "That's not fair. *No way!*"

TWENTY-ONE

The cheering stopped. A hush fell over the auditorium.

"Frankie, what's your problem?" Wacky Jackie asked.

Frankie pointed at the five new kids. "Those Garbage Pail Kids over there can't just show up at the last minute and win the same as us. I don't want them to come to Six Thrills with us," he said.

"Why?" Jackie demanded.

"Because they're fake."

"Your brain is fake!" Nasty Nancy shouted at Frankie.

Brett Sweat picked up the black cat and mopped sweat off his forehead with it. By the time Brett was finished, the cat was dripping wet.

"Who are the fakes?" Brett demanded. "And who aren't the fakes? We know who *we* are. But who are *you*?"

"Who are I?" Wacky Jackie replied. "Don't you mean, who am you?"

"Who am you?" Brett said. "That's what I'm asking. I know who I are. But is you who?"

"You're not me!" Wacky Jackie exclaimed. "So who am I?"

"Who am me?" Brett Sweat replied. "I'm asking you, who am me?"

"You is you and I am me," Jackie said.

"You're giving me a m-migraine!" Nervous Rex cried, holding his head.

Wacky Jackie frowned. "Is it *my graine*? Or is it *your graine*?"

Nat Nerd jumped back up onto the table again. "Manners, everyone. Remember your manners!" he shouted.

I gazed down. Rob Slob Junior had eaten one of the mayor's shoes. I think the mayor was too upset to notice.

I'm the brainiac in the group, so I knew it was my job to settle this argument. The contest was a tie, so everyone was going to the amusement park.

There had to be a way to make everyone happy about that.

"Okay, okay," I said, holding up both hands. "You fake Garbage Pail Kids are welcome to come along with us to Six Thrills. But we'll have a better time than you!"

"Huh?"

"Wha—?"

"Excuse me?"

Nasty Nancy shook her head. "We'll have a better time than you with our eyes closed!" she said.

"Don't shut your eyes—just shut your mouth!" Cranky Frankie snapped.

"Manners, everyone! Manners," Nat Nerd called from on top of the table.

Patty Perfect stuck her perfect nose in the air. "Peter and *I* will have the best time!" she said. "That's because we are perfectly happy wherever we go."

"We always have a perfectly awesome time because we are perfect!" her brother exclaimed.

"Your dog ran away. Who says you get to go?" Cranky Frankie exclaimed.

"Yea," Nasty Nancy agreed. "Mind your own business."

I could see another fight was about to start. I knew I had to think quickly to stop it. But thankfully, quick thinking is what I'm known for. My quick thinking is quicker than anyone else's quick thinking.

"How about a contest?" I said.

Windy Winston squinted at me. "Another pet contest?"

"No," I said. "A contest to see who has the best time."

They all muttered to themselves. I'm not sure what they were saying, but I think they were talking about how brilliant I am.

"We'll give out points at each ride and each game and each food place," I said. "Points for having the best time. And we'll see who *really* has the best time."

"I'm already having a great time," Babbling Brooke said. "I got a head start on all of you!"

"Nobody puts Peter and Patty Perfect in the corner. We started having a good time yesterday," Peter Perfect said. "So we're going, too. And we're already winning— *big time*."

"Let's start the contest at the amusement park," I said. "Everyone agree?"

"I know who I are," Brett Sweat said. "But who am you?"

TWENTY-TWO

As we were walking home, I had a lot of brilliant ideas about how we could have the best time at Six Thrills Amusement Park. My brainiest idea was for each of us to carry a feather. That way we could tickle one another all the time and we would keep laughing.

But no one seemed to like that idea.

"Feathers make me sneeze," Wacky Jackie said.

"I'm not ticklish. Tickling makes me puke," Luke Puke said.

"I'm scared of feathers," Nervous Rex said. "I always wonder where they came from. Did someone pull them off a bird? Did it hurt to have their feathers p-plucked out?"

"Okay, okay," I said. "Forget the feathers. Here's another brilliant idea. Whenever we go on a ride, we don't get off when it's over. We go around six times for every ride. How much fun would *that* be?"

"I always puke on rides," Luke Puke said.

"Rides make me nervous," said Nervous Rex. "I'm always thinking, when will the ride end? How much longer will it go? And, what if the ride never stops?"

"I get hungry on long rides," Junkfood John chimed in. "Once, I was on a very long roller coaster ride and I just kept thinking about tortilla chips and salsa. I know other people were laughing and screaming, but I couldn't hear them because my belly was growling too loud."

"Come on, guys," I pleaded. "We're a fun group—aren't we? We love to have fun. And I know we can have the most fun of anybody at the park!"

"YAY, JANEY!"

Babbling Brooke clapped her hands, leapt in the air, and performed a cheer.

"YAY, JANEY, YAY, JANEY,
"YOU'RE SO BRAINY!
"BUT WE DON'T LIKE YOUR
    IDEAS,
"WE THINK THEY ARE LAMEY!
"YAAAAY!"

She did a backward somersault and fell down an open manhole.

"Okay, okay, I get it," I said, rolling my eyes. "You don't like those ideas. Let's have a meeting when we get home and talk about how we're going to win the contest."

"We can't," Junkfood John and Rob Slob said at the same time. "No meeting today."

"Why not?" I asked.

"Because we have to watch *The Mighty Hairball*," Rob answered. "He got his own TV series, and the first episode is on this afternoon."

"The Mighty Hairball joined the League of Sidekicks," John said. "And his new show is on the Sidekick Channel."

"But how can the Hairball fight crime without Jonny Pantsfalldown and his Pants of Steel?" I asked.

"It's gonna be awesome!" Rob Slob declared. "For one thing, in the new series, the Mighty Hairball *doesn't wear pants!*"

Episode 1

Get ready for a *HAIRY* adventure, everyone, as the world's mightiest sidekick lurches off on his own to fight crime, bad people, and bad stuff wherever he finds it! *"I spit on crime!"* is the Hairball's motto. And when he spits, criminals better duck!

Don't look away!

It's me, the Mighty Hairball, and I just sneezed all over my face. I'm allergic to my costume, and this happens a lot. As you can see, I'm wiping the snot away with my Official Hairball Handkerchief—made of real hair—which is available on my website, BigLoser.com.

I know, it's a bad name for a website. But all the good ones are taken.

You may think that as a supersidekick, my life is one thrill after another. But you'd be wrong. Right now I have a big problem.

Like what to do with a snotty handkerchief when I don't wear pants and there are no pockets in my costume? I can't just stand here holding it. Where can I put it?

I guess I'll tuck it under my shirt. **UGH**. It's all slimy.

That's one thing they don't teach you at Sidekick School.

But I can't worry about that now. I have bad guys and bad things to fight.

I'm on my own now. My partner, Jonny Pantsfalldown, was hurt in a very bad toilet accident.

When he regained consciousness, he asked me to defend the good people of Pupick Falls with all my Hairball strength. And I'm ready to do whatever it takes—especially if it means I have my own TV series.

Oh, wait. A knock at the door. Someone in trouble has come for my help.

It's a young woman wearing a gray hoodie that almost covers her entire face. "Come in," I say. "I'm the Mighty Hairball."

"You look like yourself," she says. "I need your help."

"How did you find me?" I ask.

"There's a sign on your front door," she explains. "It says, SECRET HIDEOUT."

"Oh, right," I say. "Maybe I should change that. What's your name?"

"My name is Anonymous," she says.

I squint at her. "How do you spell that?"

She shrugs. "I'm not sure."

"You can't spell your own name?"

"A lot of people can't spell it."

"Tell me your problem," I say. "And don't worry, Anonymous. No case is too tough for me. I spit on crime."

"I notice you have a little drool on your chin," she says.

I wiped it off with the front of my cape.

"It's kind of a long story. Are you taking notes?" she asks.

"I can't take notes," I say. "I don't have a place for a pencil. My costume doesn't have pockets."

The woman frowned. "I'll try to keep it short then. You see, I can't sleep at night."

"And you want me to come over and sing lullabies to you?" I asked.

She pulled the hoodie over her head, as if she wanted to hide. "No, you hairball," she said. "I can't sleep at night because of the owl fights."

"Owl fights?" I cried. "Owl fights are illegal in Pupick Falls!"

"Tell that to Little Tookus," she said. "Little Tookus stages owl fights outside my house every night."

Hearing that name made my hair stand on end like in a cartoon.

Little Tookus.

Little Tookus is my archenemy. He is a bad dude. He's so bad, he wears a T-shirt that says SO WHAT? on the front.

"Do you think you can find Little Tookus?" she asked.

"He's easy to find," I told her. "He has the tiniest tookus in town."

I felt the excitement of my first adventure.

I jumped to my feet and spit in the air. "Oh. Sorry," I said. "Did I get you?"

THE MIGHTY HAIRBALL CONTINUED...

" The owl fights go on all night," Anonymous said. "And all the cheering and shouting from the crowd keeps me awake."

"Owl fights are very exciting," I said. "I once won one myself."

The young woman squinted at me. "You fought an owl?"

"It wasn't a fair fight," I said. "But I needed the birdseed."

She blinked. "But . . . you aren't an owl."

I nodded. "That's why I had to give it up. They took away my owl-fighting license. So I went to Sidekick School instead."

"Did anyone ever tell you you are very boring?" she asked.

"No," I said. "But thank you. Now let's go after Little Tookus and break up the owl fights in front of your house."

She hurried to the front door of my not-so-secret headquarters. "Hairball, are you going to fly?"

I shook my head. "No, I get airsick. We'll have to walk."

I pulled down my winged helmet and swept my official 60 percent cotton, hairlined cape behind me. And remember, the official Hairball cape is available on my website, BigLoser.com.

I stepped outside and began to take long superhero-sidekick strides along the road to town.

"It's a very long walk," she said.

"I don't care," I said. "I *spit* at long walks!" I spit into the air. "Oh . . . sorry. Did I get you again?"

"I have a car," the young woman said. "I'll meet you there."

"Can you give me a ride?" I asked.

I guess she didn't hear me, because she took off with a roar and didn't look back.

Two days later, I arrived at the site of Little Tookus's owl fights. A big, cheering crowd had

gathered in front of a card table. And two owls were going at it, pecking at each other's midsections, headbutting, and winging the other with unspeakable violence.

I didn't hesitate. I strode right over to Little Tookus and shoved my face up to his. "Are you Little Tookus?" I demanded.

"Who?"

"Are you the manager of these owl fights?"

"Who?"

"This fight has to stop," I said. "Do you know who I am?"

"Who?" he replied.

I suddenly realized that Little Tookus wasn't answering me. It was one of the owls.

"Little Tookus, these owl fights must stop at once!" I demanded.

He sneered at me. "Who says?"

"I do. I'm the Mighty Hairball."

"Who?"

This time it wasn't the owl.

"The Mighty Hairball," I replied.

"Who cares?"

"Little Tookus, will you stop these fights?"

"Who knows?"

Cheers went up as one of the fighting owls toppled off the table.

"We have a winner!" Little Tookus declared. He raised the winning owl above his head. "Next challenger! Let's have the next fighting owl on the table!"

I grabbed the evil villain by the shoulders. "I can have your card table folded up and taken away," I said.

"Who cares?"

"These fights are against the law."

"Who says?"

"You don't realize who you are talking to!" I exclaimed.

"Who?"

"You can't talk to me like that!" I cried. "I'm the Mighty Hairball. I *spit* on crime!"

I puckered my lips to spit—but Little Tookus clamped a hand over my mouth.

"*Mmmmumph mummmmph mummmph*," I said.

He squeezed my face so hard, I think I swallowed a few teeth. "My owl fights are going to go on every night, Hairball," he growled. "And there is nothing *you* can do about it!"

THE MIGHTY HAIRBALL CONTINUED...

Little Tookus let go of my face and asked me a question: *"So what are you going to do, Hairball?"*

I stepped back, rubbing the pain from my cheeks. "Nothing," I told him.

He glared at me. "You're going to do nothing?"

I nodded. "Yes. Nothing."

He eyed me suspiciously. "What are you saying? You're not going to do anything about my illegal owl fights?"

"That's right," I answered. "I can't do anything, Little Tookus. Because I'm just a sidekick, not a superhero. I don't have any powers. And as a sworn and licensed sidekick, I'm not allowed to do anything at all."

Tookus gave me a hard shove. "Then step back," he growled. "You're blocking everyone's view of the next fight."

As the next two owls began dancing around the card table, pecking at each other, I walked away. I had a lot to think about—especially about my career path and my crime-fighting future.

The young woman named Anonymous was waiting for me across the street.

"Sorry," I muttered. "The Mighty Hairball couldn't stop the fights after all."

"That's okay," she said. "I think I'm going to move to Abu Dhabi. I hear they don't have any owls over there." From under her hoodie, she flashed me a smile. "Thanks for your help."

"No thanks needed," I said. "I fight crime wherever I see it. The Mighty Hairball *spits* on crime!"

I puckered my lips and spit into the air.

"Oh, sorry. Did I get you again?"

Keep your lips puckered for more adventure, everyone! The Mighty Hairball will return next week for another tale of thrilling sidekick action! In the meantime, be safe, be strong . . . and spit on crime whenever you can!

TWENTY-THREE

Brainy Janey here to continue the story . . .

Junkfood John and Rob Slob looked at one another and shrugged.

"Hmmmm," John said. "Sometimes it takes a show a while to hit its stride."

"I guess," Rob said, turning off the TV.

"I thought it was *awesome*," Babbling Brooke said. But there's very little that Brooke doesn't like. She enjoys staring at cheese in the refrigerator.

At any rate, things were about to get *really* exciting because a week later we were all on a big yellow bus heading to Six Thrills Amusement Park, and we were going to have a better time than anyone else.

We are all wearing special T-shirts. I ordered white ones for everyone with black letters on the front that say: WE'RE THE BEST.

The T-shirt maker made a mistake—because when we opened the package, the shirts all had an extra letter. So the shirts say: WE'RE THE BEAST. But that's okay.

Maybe it's even better.

No one could sleep last night—we were too excited. So we arrived at the bus early in the morning.

The door was open, and I climbed onboard two steps at a time. But I let out a startled cry when I saw Patty and Peter Perfect sitting in the first two seats.

"We got here last night," Patty said. "We wanted to be sure to sit up front. You know, because it's the most fun."

"We should get ten points for sitting in the most fun seats," Peter Perfect added. "We're already having the most *awesome* time."

"We're even having fun waiting here, and it's been *hours*," Patty said. "Because we're perfect. By the way, do you like our T-shirts. They're handmade. I'll bet you can't guess what the P is for."

I ignored her. "Where is the bus driver?" I asked.

"We haven't seen the driver yet," Peter answered. "But we're having the most fun anyway."

I took a seat behind the Perfects, and the others began to pile in.

Nervous Rex was trembling and grabbed the back of my seat. "Buses make me nervous," he said. "I never know which is the sunny side and which is the shady side."

"Why do you care?" I asked.

"I don't," he said. "It's just something else to worry about."

Junkfood John squeezed onto the bus and started down the narrow aisle. He carried a large red bowl in front of him. "What's in the bowl?" I asked.

"It's this new snack food," John said. "They're called *grapes*." He popped a few into his mouth.

"Grapes?" Nervous Rex asked.

John nodded. "Yeah. They're weird. They don't have any chocolate or nuts or salt on them or anything. They're very squishy. Although sometimes they crunch."

"Those are the seeds," I told him. "You know, grapes are a *fruit*."

John scrunched up his face. "Fruit? What's *fruit*?"

"Did you ever eat an apple or an orange or a banana?" I asked.

He shook his head. "No. I pretty much just eat stuff that comes in cartons or plastic bags."

"Why did you bring those grapes with you?" Nervous Rex asked him.

Junkfood John shrugged. "I thought they might be fun to throw at people. But I've already eaten half of them."

Rob Slob grabbed a handful of grapes from the bowl. He raised them high in the air and squeezed the juice onto John's head. "Hey, cool," Rob said. "This snack makes juice."

John wiped his hair with one hand. "Why did you do that?"

Rob Slob shrugged. "I don't know. I just did it."

Adam Bomb climbed onto the bus next. "Are we having fun yet?" he asked. He squeezed beside me and took the window seat.

It always takes Adam a day or two to get himself together after he explodes. I was glad he came back in time for our trip to Six Thrills.

Junkfood John tossed a grape at Wacky Jackie. She caught it between her teeth and spit it back at him. "I knew these things called grapes would be fun!" John exclaimed.

Jackie stopped beside my seat and made a face. "Look, Janey. My T-shirt doesn't fit at all."

I studied it. Then I rolled my eyes. "Jackie, you put it on upside down," I said.

"Oh, thank goodness!" she said, and laughed. "I thought I was standing on my head."

"How do you put a T-shirt on upside down?" I asked her.

"It takes work."

"It's also inside out," I said.

Jackie frowned. "Does it really make a difference?"

The bus driver's seat was still empty. "Has anyone seen the driver?" I asked.

No one answered.

"Peter and I are having the most fun waiting for him!" Patty Perfect called from the front seat. "We're having the *best* time. Ten more points for us! Yaaay."

Adam Bomb poked me in the side and pointed out the window. "Uh-oh," he murmured. "Here comes trouble."

TWENTY-FOUR

I leaned over Adam and peered out the window. The *other* Garbage Pail Kids had arrived.

Windy Winston stepped onto the bus and waved at everyone. "The party can start now," he said. "The Big Five are here!"

Junkfood John bounced a grape off Winston's head.

"Check this out!" Winston shouted. He stuck out his chest so we could all see his T-shirt. It said: BEST TIME NEVER!

"It's supposed to say 'best time ever!,'" Winston said. "But the T-shirt place messed up." He sighed. "We're all wearing it anyway because our other shirts are dirty."

Nasty Nancy followed him down the bus aisle and made a disgusted face. "Why does this bus smell so bad?" she groaned.

"It didn't—until you got on!" Cranky Frankie exclaimed.

"No fighting," Nat Nerd scolded. "We're here to have the best time, so let's all remember our manners!"

Cranky Frankie stuck a leg out and tripped him. Nat Nerd fell on his face.

"No worries," he cried, and pulled himself up. "No worries. I'm having the best time. Plus, I think I should get ten points for falling down and still having fun!"

"Is it hot in here or is it me?" Brett Sweat asked. His face was dripping. He grabbed Wacky Jackie's T-shirt and mopped his sweat with it.

"Hey—" Jackie protested.

Brett Sweat blinked. "Oh, is that your shirt? Sorry, I thought it was a towel."

"Remember, we're here to have fun!" Nat Nerd called from the back of the bus.

"I put my T-shirt on upside down," Jackie told him.

"That's funny," Brett replied. "This morning I put my jeans on upside down and fell out the window!"

"That happens," Jackie said.

Disgustin' Justin pulled himself onto the bus. He had dark stains all over the front of his BEST TIME NEVER! T-shirt.

123

"Hey, Justin," Cranky Frankie called. "Is that your breakfast all over your shirt?"

Justin scowled angrily and waved a fist. "No, *you're* my breakfast!"

Cranky Frankie sank back in his seat. "Just asking," he said softly.

"I don't even know how I got these gross stains on my shirt," Justin growled. "That how disgustin' I am!"

"We like you anyway!" Brett Sweat said.

"No, we don't!" Nasty Nancy chimed in.

Disgustin' Justin stopped beside Junkfood John. Justin grabbed a grape from his bowl and pushed it up John's left nostril.

"Hey!" John cried. "Why'd you shove a grape up my nose?"

"Who says I did?" Justin replied, leaning over Junkfood John.

"You did too! And you know you did!" John exclaimed.

"Can you prove it?" Justin asked.

"Of course I can prove it," John said. "I have a grape up my nose. Why'd you do it?"

Disgustin' Justin shrugged. "Just having fun. We're supposed to be having fun, right? And so far, I'm having more fun than you. So ten points for me."

Junkfood John shook his head. "I'm just glad I didn't bring a pineapple!" he muttered, then snorted out the grape and ate it.

I glanced at the time. "Hey, everyone, we're late," I yelled. "We were supposed to leave for the amusement park ten minutes ago."

"But where's our driver?" Adam Bomb asked, looking out the window.

"Yea, where's our driver?" I repeated.

"Where's our driver? Where's our driver? Where's our driver?" Handy Sandy, Luke Puke, and Babbling Brooke began to chant.

Then I heard a roaring sound. "Hey, look!" I cried, and pointed out the window at the yellow school bus that came rumbling past us.

An *empty* yellow school bus.

A school bus with just a driver in the front. And row after row of empty seats.

It raced past us and picked up speed as it disappeared ahead.

Even though I'm a brainiac, it took me a few seconds to figure out what had happened.

"Guess what, guys?" I said. "We got on the *wrong bus.*"

TWENTY-FIVE

Mayor Crumbum had to make all new plans for us. Two days later, we were ready once again to set off for Six Thrills Amusement Park.

The night before, we had a house meeting. "We don't want Patty and Peter Perfect to sit in the first row on the bus," Adam Bomb said. "They had too good of a time."

Everyone agreed. We definitely didn't want the Perfects to win the contest.

Adam turned to me. "Janey, you're the brainiac. How can we keep the Perfects from getting in the front seat?"

I thought about it for ten minutes. "What if we get there early and *take out* the front seat?" I said.

"Awwwwk. Brilliant!" Ptooey squawked from his perch. **"Brilliant for a *bird brain*!"**

Handy Sandy raised her hand. "Uh . . . Janey," she said, "I think it's a pretty good idea. But if we take out the front row of seats, doesn't the second row of seats become the first row?"

I thought about it for a while. "So, Sandy, what you're saying is we should take out *all* the seats? That would definitely keep Peter and Patty from taking the ones up front."

"Awwwwk. Ptooey! Brilliant! Brilliant! Come here and take a bow. I'll peck your head off!"

Babbling Brooke looked confused. "If we take out all the seats," she said, "where would we hide them? I guess we could hide them on the bus, right?"

Luke Puke grabbed his belly. "All this talk is making me feel sick," he said. "You know I get bus sick." Then he jumped up and ran from the room.

"I think I know what we should do," Handy Sandy said. "Get there really early tomorrow morning—before the Perfects show up. And pour water all over the front seats. There's *no way* they'll want to sit on them then."

"That's an awesome idea!" I exclaimed, and clapped Sandy on the back. "That's the kind of smart idea *I* would think of!"

So that's what we did.

We all trooped to the bus stop before dawn. It was still pitch-black out. The sun wouldn't rise for at least an hour.

We crept up to the bus, which was dark and silent.

Cranky Frankie carried a bucket of water and climbed the steps onto the bus. Then he tilted the bucket and let all the water pour onto the front seats.

I climbed up behind him. "Good job," I whispered.

And then we heard a shout from the back of the bus. "Hey, good morning! Isn't it a *perfect* morning?"

I raised my gaze—and saw Patty and Peter Perfect. They were smiling and waving to us from the back row of the bus.

"We got here early," Peter Perfect shouted. "Because we wanted to get the *back seats.*"

"The back seats are the most fun!" Patty Perfect called. "All those bumps and turns. Peter and I are already having the best time because we got the back seats!"

"I guess we score even *more* points," Peter added.

I let out a sigh and took a seat by the window. Cranky Frankie tossed the empty bucket off the bus and sat down beside me, shaking his head.

The rest of our gang climbed on and found seats. And a few minutes later, the five new kids showed up and squeezed onto the bus.

When everyone was on board, Handy Sandy jumped to her feet. "I'm going to judge the contest to see who has the best time," she said. "Because I'm handy with numbers."

"Who's winning?" Windy Winston demanded.

"We're starting today from zero, so the Perfect twins have twenty points," Sandy answered. "No one else has any."

The Perfect twins jumped up and cheered for themselves. They stopped when a young man in a gray uniform climbed onto the bus.

He tipped his cap. "I'm Andrew, your driver," he said. "Good morning, everyone!"

"Good morning, Andrew!" we called back.

"Let's get going to Six Thrills!" he said.

And we all cheered.

Andrew turned and lowered himself into the driver's seat.

Then froze for a moment.

He blinked several times.

"Hey!" he cried! "Hey! Hey! Hey! Hey! Who poured *water* all over my seat?"

He jumped up and turned to us angrily. His face darkened to red and an angry scowl spread over it.

"Who did it? Who soaked my driver's seat in water?" he demanded.

Beside me, Cranky Frankie lowered his head and tried to duck out of sight. "Oh wow," he murmured. "I did the wrong seat."

Andrew furiously slammed his cap against the bus door. "Well, good luck to you kids," he shouted. "I'm not driving you anywhere!"

Then he stomped off the bus and disappeared down the street.

Wacky Jackie jumped to her feet. "Are we having fun yet?" she asked.

TWENTY-SIX

Three days later, we were all on the big yellow school bus, and we were finally on our way to Six Thrills Amusement Park.

This time, we decided to do nothing. Nothing at all. We sat in our seats quietly and behaved like angels so we could actually make it to the park.

Patty and Peter Perfect were sitting in the middle seats—they said the middle seats were the most fun. They were still winning the contest. But I knew things would change once we reached the park.

I knew our guys could have the best time of anyone because we always have the best time. Even when our teacher, Mrs. Hooping-Koff, keeps us after school for having too good of a time in class.

I turned to Babbling Brooke, who sat beside me. "What's your favorite ride at Six Thrills?" I asked.

Brooke thought for a few seconds. "I guess the Tilt-a-Tilt," she said. "I like the way you get tilted and then when you think you're through tilting, you get tilted some more."

"Do you know what ride makes me barf?" Luke Puke asked.

I turned to him. "No . . . what ride?"

"This *bus ride*," he said. He made an **ULP** sound and cupped his hands over his mouth.

"Do you know what's the most fun?" Windy Winston said. "The Swirl-a-Fly Twirl High 'n' Float Away ride."

"I've never been on it," I said. "What does it do?"

"A rope comes down and lifts you off the ground," Winston answered. "Then it whirls you high above the ground and flings you into a tree. You climb down the trunk, grab another rope, and are flung back into the air and you have no idea where you're gonna land."

"Whooa! Hold on!" Adam Bomb exclaimed. "Why is *that* the most fun ride?"

"Because I just made it up," Winston said.

"Winston, you're seriously waaay weird," Nasty Nancy said. "And I don't mean that as a compliment."

"It takes one to know one!" Winston shot back.

"Hey, no arguing!" the driver called from the front.

"No arguing," Adam Bomb repeated, staring at Nasty

Nancy and Windy Winston. "We want to make it to the park this time so we can start having a better time than the rest of you."

"Peter and I are having the *best* time sitting in the middle row!" Patty Perfect shouted. "Too bad you all can't sit in the middle row with us! We each have a window seat and room to spread our legs"

The bus suddenly lurched hard and threw us all back against our seats as it came to a stop.

The driver opened the door and turned back to us. "Here you go, people!" he shouted. "Last stop. Six Thrills Amusement Park. Have a thrilling day, everyone!"

We all pushed and shoved our way down the narrow bus aisle and jumped off. It was a sunny, beautiful, warm day. I followed everyone to the entrance booth and could feel my heart start to patter with excitement.

We pulled out our free passes and jammed together in front of the ticket booth. "Hey, there's no one in here," Brett Sweat said.

The booth was dark and empty.

"How do we get in?" Adam Bomb asked. "There's nobody here to let us inside."

Adam's face was as red as a tomato. I hoped he wasn't about to explode.

Finally, a man in a white uniform carrying a long broom appeared at the side of the booth. He looked surprised to see us.

"We won free passes," Adam Bomb explained. "Can you let us in?"

The man shook his head. "No can do . . . sorry. The park is closed on Mondays."

BRAINY JANEY'S BRAIN-TEASER MATH QUIZ

While you're waiting to see if the kids ever get to Six Thrills Amusement Park, you can take Brainy Janey's super-fun math quiz. (Her answers are at the end. Don't peek!)

QUESTIONS

1. If I have two ham sandwiches and you give me four ham sandwiches, what will you eat for lunch?

2. If Train A leaves the station at 2:00 going 60 miles per hour, and Train B leaves the station at 3:00 going 100 miles per hour, why did you decide to take the bus?

3. How do you write the number 600 in numbers?

4. If I divide a chicken into three parts, and I take away one part, will it rain on Tuesday?

5. A salmon swims upstream at 20 miles per hour and downstream at 30 miles per hour. How long will it take it to get to Cincinnati?

6. Four + infinity =

7. If an apple falls from an apple tree every six minutes, then what?

8. If I have two peanut butter sandwiches and you have two jelly sandwiches, what happened to your ham sandwiches?

ANSWERS

1. Pizza.

2. I don't know.

3. 600 in numbers.

4. The forecast calls for partly cloudy.

5. Beats me.

6. A very high number.

7. Then I guess I'd better be careful where I walk.

8. I ate the ham sandwiches and then I swam upstream to Cincinnati.

TWENTY-SEVEN

Nasty Nancy here. I'm continuing the story, whether you like it or not.

My four friends and I were happy to meet the other ten kids who call themselves the Garbage Pail Kids. It's great to know there are other kids in town who are normal and good-looking like us.

Of course, they're not as normal *or* as good-looking as we are.

We are the *real* Garbage Pail Kids. We live together in a big old house behind a row of garbage cans. We have no parents, but we get along just fine without them.

I call those other ten kids the Garbage Pail Punk-Faced-Brat-Nose-Dim-Bulb-Lame-Brain-Snot-Head Kids.

And I mean it in a good way.

I know I'm being too kind to them. But I'm a

kind person. I can never understand why idiots and dumbheads call me Nasty Nancy.

Anyway, a week later, we all climbed on the yellow school bus once again to try to get to Six Thrills Amusement Park. Those two freaks, the Perfect twins, decided to stand up this time. They said it was "the most fun way to ride a bus."

The Perfects wanted extra points for standing up. But the contest scorekeeper, the girl named Handy Sandy, refused. She waved a little notepad in the air. "I'm not keeping score this time until we get to the park," she said.

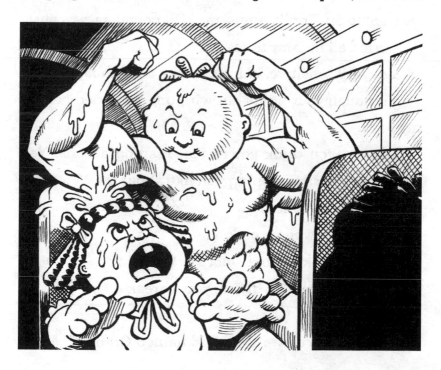

I sat next to Brett Sweat. Guess what? He was sweating like a lawn sprinkler.

He turned to me. "Nancy, is it hot in here—or is it just me?"

I pinched two fingers over my nose. "Brett, I have an awesome Christmas present for you," I said.

His eyes went wide. "A present? For me? What is it?"

"Deodorant," I said.

He wiped his face off on the sleeve of my T-shirt.

I'm hoping my four friends and I have the best time of everyone and win the contest. But I was worried. Last year, we went to Six Thrills Amusement Park and it was a bust.

I cried all the way home.

I'm very sensitive. Want to make something of it?

I'll punch your lights out with one hand tied behind my back.

I know, you think you're just reading a book. You think you can say anything you like about me. You think you're perfectly safe.

But I know where you live.

So don't look around. Just keep reading.

But remember. I'm giving you a break. I won't *always* be this nice.

"Where's the driver?" the kid named Cranky Frankie

yelled from the back of the bus. "We've been trying to get to Six Thrills for *weeks!*"

A woman stepped onto the bus and waved to everyone with a big smile. She carried a picnic basket in one hand and an umbrella in the other.

"Are you the driver?" I asked.

She shook her head. "No, I'm Mrs. Hooping-Koff. I'm their teacher," she said, motioning to the other kids.

A bald man in a baggy brown suit stepped up behind her. "For those who don't know him, this is Principal Grunt," Mrs. Hooping-Koff shouted. "That isn't his real

name. But we all call him that because he only grunts. For the life of us, we can't understand a word he says!"

The principal nodded. *"Grunnnt grunt grunnnnt!"* he exclaimed.

"Principal Grunt and I are at Smellville Middle School," the teacher continued. "Where do you kids go to school?"

"We're at Urrrrrp Academy," Nat Nerd told her.

"Someone burped while they were naming our school," I explained.

"Grunt gruntgruntgrunt," the principal said.

"How come the two of you are here?" Cranky Frankie called to them.

"We are your chaperones," Mrs. Hooping-Koff answered. "Does anyone know what 'chaperone' means?"

The girl named Brainy Janey raised her hand. "It means 'hat' in Spanglish," she said. "The person who wears the hat is always the leader."

"Grunnnnnt," the principal said.

"That's not quite right," Mrs. Hooping-Koff replied. "We two chaperones are going with you to make sure you have a good time—but not a *really good* time."

"Peter and I are going to have the *best* time," Patty Perfect said.

"Standing up on the bus is the *best*," Peter Perfect chimed in. "Patty and I are going to get extra credit for standing."

"No. No you're not," Handy Sandy said, waving her notepad in the air.

Mrs. Hooping-Koff grabbed the pad from her. "I'll be the scorekeeper," she said. "That's a chaperone's job."

She and the principal took seats in the middle so they could keep an eye on all of us. "I'm giving Peter and Patty Perfect ten extra points," she announced, scribbling on the notepad. "Look how well groomed they are."

Big smiles burst across the Perfect twins' faces. "We always try to look perfect," Patty said.

"Patty and I brushed each other's hair this morning," Peter said.

Patty grinned. "And we didn't even use brushes."

I wanted to gag.

Do we really have to spend the whole day with *those two*?

Please. Somebody put me out of my misery.

"WHOOOAH!"

Everyone let out a cry as the bus jerked forward. We fell back in our seats and watched as we pulled away from the curb.

"Finally!" I cried. "We're on our way!"

Brett Sweat wiped his face on my sleeve. "Is it hot in here or is it me?" he asked.

The bus squealed and swerved. We were all tossed from one side to the other.

"Does everyone have their seat belts fastened?" Mrs. Hooping-Koff asked.

I searched around on the seat. "There aren't any!" I called out.

"Then just pretend," she replied.

Seriously?

Another squeal. Another shriek of the brakes. Another terrifying *jolt*.

The bus bounced off something and then roared back into traffic.

Some of the kids were screaming.

I shut my eyes!

The driver gave a long horn blast—and the bus swerved in a crazy zigzag.

I kept my eyes shut and gripped the back of the seat in front of me with both hands.

I heard a crash. Shattering glass. A hard bump. The bus roared on.

Finally, after what seemed like an eternity, we came

to a hard, teeth-clamping stop. I froze for a long moment, afraid to open my eyes.

"We're here!" someone shouted. "Yaaaaay. We made it. We're here."

I slowly opened my eyes. Then stood up on shaky legs and started to the front.

Who was the driver? Who was that grinning kid sitting behind the wheel?

It was the girl they call Wacky Jackie.

Mrs. Hooping-Koff's eyes bulged. *"You? YOU* were the one driving?!" she gasped.

Jackie nodded. "I got tired of waiting."

"But—but—but—" the teacher sputtered.

"I always wondered if I could drive a bus!" Jackie said.

I flashed her a thumbs-up. "Good job," I said.

I was being sarcastic, but I don't think she noticed.

I followed everyone off the bus and into the parking lot. The bumpers and fenders of the bus were totally battered and bent. I was just glad to be in one piece.

We all began to walk toward the ticket booth. But then we stopped—and read the sign above the entrance:

EIGHT SCREAMS AMUSEMENT PARK

That's right. Wacky Jackie took us to the *wrong park.*

TWENTY-EIGHT

Adam Bomb again, taking over the telling of this story. And what a story it's been. But I'm happy to say, one week later, we all arrived at Six Thrills Amusement Park. With a real bus driver, too. We paraded through the turnstiles at the front gate and stood at the entryway, staring at all the rides and restaurants and attractions.

"We're here! We're here!" Babbling Brooke gushed. Then she leaped into the air and began a cheer:

"WE'RE HERE! WE'RE HERE!

"WE CAME FROM FAR AND
  NEAR!

"GIVE ME AN F!

"GIVE ME A U!

"GIVE ME AN N-N!

"WHAT HAVE WE GOT?

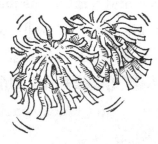

"FUNN!

"YAAAAY!"

Brooke did a flying cartwheel and landed on the top of her skull. Handy Sandy and Nervous Rex carried her to the medical building.

Mrs. Hooping-Koff scratched her head. "F-U-N-N?" she murmured.

"You know, Brooke has never been a very good speller," I said. "But she has a lot of spirit."

"*Grunnnnnt,*" our principal agreed.

Mrs. Hooping-Koff turned and gazed at Rob Slob. "Rob, how did you get that mud all over your shoes?"

Rob looked down. "I'm not wearing shoes," he said.

"Let's get on a ride!" Windy Winston shouted. "We can't stand here all day."

"Patty and I are having the best time standing here!" Peter Perfect exclaimed.

"We love standing here," his sister agreed. "Mrs. Hooping-Koff, give us ten points for that."

Mrs. Hooping-Koff took out the little scorepad and scribbled down ten points for the Perfects. She thinks they're perfect and will do anything they say.

"There's the Tilt-a-Tilt," Brett Sweat said, pointing. Even his pointer finger was sweating! "Let's do it!"

"I don't like the Tilt-a-Tilt," Luke Puke said. "It's too tilty. I get Tilt-a-Sick."

"How about the Buzz Saw?" Windy Winston asked. "It's like a log ride. Your log rolls down the river, a buzz saw cuts it in half, and you swim to the finish."

"We can't do a water ride," Nat Nerd said. "I forgot my bathing suit."

"Peter and I brought extra bathing suits," Patty Perfect chimed in.

"We can loan you one," Peter Perfect said. He turned to Mrs. Hooping-Koff. "Do we get extra points for that?"

She scribbled ten extra points for that in her notepad.

"We are having the best time arguing about the different rides," Patty Perfect gushed.

Mrs. Hooping-Koff awarded them ten more points.

"Does anyone want some Honey Crunch Tree Bark?" Junkfood John asked. He held up a big brown bag and was chewing loudly.

"We already had breakfast, John," I said.

He shrugged. "I know. But this is a snack." He waved the bag in the air. "Anyone want to try some? It's made from real tree bark. No artificial flavors."

"Grunnnt gruntgrunt," the principal grunted. We had no idea what he was trying to say.

"There's the Whip-It Swing Ride!" Handy Sandy cried. "That's a fun, simple ride to start out on."

Sandy was right. The Whip-It was just swing seats on very long cords. The ride swung you around and around, and your swing floated out higher as you spun. Then, suddenly, it would stop and whip you in the other direction and your seat would fly even higher.

It was simple but fun, so we all started trotting toward it.

"We love the Whip-It!" Patty Perfect exclaimed. "We'll have the best time of everyone on this terrifying—I mean—terrific ride."

Mrs. Hooping-Koff wrote in her notebook again.

I shook my head. "We're never going to beat the Perfects unless we cheat," I muttered.

"Don't worry," Cranky Frankie said, running up beside me. "I thought of that. That's why I brought this can of grease."

TWENTY-NINE

I stopped and stared at the small can Frankie held in front of me.

"It's called Greasy Grease," Frankie whispered, keeping the can close to his body so no one else could see it. "It's the greasiest grease you can buy without a prescription."

"But—but—" I stuttered.

He grinned. "I know what you're going to ask, Adam. You're going to ask me what am I going to do with it?"

Kids were climbing into the swing seats, getting ready to ride.

"Before the Perfect twins sit down," Cranky Frankie whispered, "I'm going to grease their seats."

I gasped. "Huh? And then—?"

Frankie's grin grew wider. "And then, when the

swings suddenly *whip* in the other direction, the Perfects will slide off their swing seats and go flying."

"But—but—"

"Believe me," Frankie whispered. "They won't have *any* fun. And they won't get any *points*, either."

"But y-you can't do that!" I stammered.

"Watch me," Frankie said.

I watched him run up to the two swings in the middle of the ride. He made sure no one was watching, then poured some Greasy Grease on his hands—and wiped them onto both seats.

"Hurry, everyone!" Mrs. Hooping-Koff shouted. "The ride is about to start! Sit down! There's room for everyone."

She and Principal Grunt found seats just as the swings started to move to the right. I gripped the two cords that held my seat and prepared to swing. I glanced down the circle of kids and saw Peter and Patty with big smiles on their perfect faces.

Cranky Frankie was in the swing beside me. He had a smile on his face, too. But it was a nasty smile.

They have a horrible surprise in store, I thought. *In a few minutes, the Perfects are going to go flying. I just hope they don't get hurt.*

The ride picked up speed. My swing and all the others floated out higher.

Kids were laughing and screaming. Everyone seemed to be having a good time.

Faster. Faster. We all swung higher. The ride moved even faster.

I held my breath. I knew what was about to happen. The ride was going to stop with a hard jolt—and then the swings would whip in the other direction.

Faster. Faster. Higher. Higher.

Here we go . . .

I wanted to close my eyes—but I couldn't.

We were flying far above the ground. Our feet were in the air, way above our heads. The swing floated out farther. And then—

WHUPPPP.

A sharp stop. The seats swung one way, then the other. Then jerked in the opposite direction.

I screamed when I saw two people slide out of their swing seats and go flying into the air.

The Perfect twins? Did the twins just go flying?

My seat swung around, so I couldn't see them.

I twisted to the side—and saw Cranky Frankie slap

his forehead. "Oh, wow. Would you *believe* it?" he cried. "I did it again. I greased the wrong seats!"

My seat whirled around—and I saw Mrs. Hooping-Koff and Principal Grunt sailing through the air.

Their mouths hung wide open in silent screams. Their hands flapped the air helplessly. They flew high over the park and then began to swoop down.

Down . . .

Down . . .

I gasped as they landed with a tall **SPLASH** into Six Thrills Lake.

Oh, wow. Oh, wow.

I hoped they could swim.

The ride ended and we all climbed off.

I felt a little dizzy.

Cranky Frankie ran to the nearest trash basket and tossed the can of grease into it. He shrugged and grinned at me. "Well, it was worth a try," he said.

The Perfect twins ran up to us. They were looking a little nauseous, but Patty Perfect said, "We had the *best* time!"

She turned to her brother. "Let's pull Mrs. Hooping-Koff out of the lake so we can tell her we won."

THIRTY

Hello, readers. I'm Windy Winston, and I'm going to continue the story of our day at Six Thrills Amusement Park.

Before I start, I'd like to tell you a little bit about me.

Do you know how I got the nickname Windy? I bet you don't. And I bet you could make ten guesses and not come up with the right answer.

You could think about it all morning and discuss it with your friends all day and dream about it at night and try to find the answer about my name online. But you won't figure it out.

So I'm going to tell you now why my nickname is Windy and save you all the trouble.

You see, people started calling me Windy because they think I talk too much.

Of course, they are wrong. That's a crazy idea. I know

when to talk and when to keep quiet. And I know I never go on and on about things and talk and talk till I'm blue in the face.

I never do that.

So I'm not sure how people got the idea that I talk too much. It was just a big mistake, and the nickname caught on, and I've been called Windy ever since.

So there you have it. Now you know.

I'm not sure about how I feel about it, to be honest. I don't want to bore you with a long discussion of my feelings. I know you'd all like to know what happened next at Six Thrills.

And, of course, I'm going to tell you all about it. So don't skip ahead. But I do feel that you should know that sometimes my nickname makes me feel a little uncomfortable.

I mean, do people *really* think I'm a windbag? That I talk too much? That I go on and on when I should just stop talking about whatever it is I'm talking about?

Do people *really* think that?

Or did they give me that nickname just to make fun of me?

If that's true, my feelings are hurt. I don't think it's nice to call someone names or give hurtful nicknames that will follow them for the rest of their life.

Do you agree with me?

I mean, Windy isn't such a bad word. But is it the right name for me? Or is my reputation being ruined because of it? Do people laugh when I tell them my name is Windy?

Sometimes I feel people are laughing behind my back. And that makes me feel really . . .

Well, I don't know how it makes me feel. I'll have to give it some thought.

I mean, what if I was called *Silent* Winston?

Would I like that better? Would it change things for me at all? Or would people still laugh when I told them my name? It's a lot to think about, as you can imagine.

But I definitely don't want to be known as someone who talks too much. Someone who just keeps talking and talking in circles. I'd be embarrassed if people thought that about me.

So I guess that explains why I'm called Windy Winston. I mean, not completely. But if you have any questions about any of this, I'm happy to discuss it more.

But now I'd like to continue the story of our adventure at Six Thrills. I'd like to—but it looks like my time is up.

Bye for now.

THIRTY-ONE

Adam Bomb here.

Whew . . . I thought that Windy Winston kid would never shut up. On the bus coming to the park, I asked him what time it was, and he talked for half an hour. I was ready to explode.

When he finished, I still didn't know what time it was—and I didn't care. I wanted to put ice cubes on my ears to cool them down from all that *listening*.

Anyway, we were all dying to ride on the park's fastest and most dangerous roller coaster, the Blister Twister. It's called that because you get blisters on your hands from squeezing the metal safety bar in front of you in terror.

The gate to the ride opened, and everyone rushed to get into a car.

Luke Puke held back. "I can't go on this ride," he said, his voice trembling.

"Because of the fast ups and downs?" I asked.

"Because it's a roller coaster," he replied, holding his stomach. "I get sick even *thinking* about roller coasters." He made an **ULLLP** sound from deep in his belly.

"You should try to get over your fear," Babbling Brooke told Luke. "Maybe you will ride the coaster and *not* get sick."

Luke Puke stared at her. "Would you like to ride in the same car with me?" he asked.

"Never mind," Brooke said. "You should probably stick with your fear. It's better for *everyone*." She then hurried into a coaster car as far away from Luke as possible.

Brainy Janey bumped up beside me. She's so smart—she was wearing gloves. That way, she wouldn't get blisters on her hands from squeezing the safety bar in terror.

"Roller coasters are so interesting," she said. "I've been studying about them."

"Why?" I asked.

She shrugged. "I don't know."

We climbed into the front car. "Roller coasters were invented by a man named Simon Roller," Janey said. "He built the first roller coaster on a beach in California."

"Interesting."

"The first coaster didn't have a car to sit in," Janey continued. "You had to pull yourself up to the top on your stomach. Then you'd do somersaults all the way down."

I shook my head. "That doesn't sound like much fun."

"Mr. Roller never got to try his own coaster," she said. "A big wave came and washed it out to sea. He forgot all about his invention and went surfing instead."

Janey is such a brainiac. She reads books in her *sleep*!

I climbed into the car beside her and pulled the metal safety bar down over our legs.

The coaster rolled forward. The Blister Twister ride was starting.

The car tilted and began to pick up speed as it rolled uphill.

Our safety bar popped back up.

"Whoa—!" I let out a cry and tugged it back down.

We climbed higher and the car picked up speed.

The safety bar popped up again.

"Oh nooo," I moaned. I stretched my hands up and tugged it down.

"STOP THE RIDE!" I screamed. "OUR SAFETY BAR IS *LOOSE*! STOP THE RIDE!"

The car zoomed up near the top.

"OUR BAR IS LOOSE!" Janey and I cried. "OUR BAR IS LOOSE! STOP THE RIDE!"

Two cars behind, Patty Perfect turned around. "LET'S ALL LET GO OF THE BAR AND RAISE OUR HANDS HIGH ABOVE OUR HEADS!" she shouted.

Brainy Janey reached up for the bar with her hands— but she missed.

We were about to go zooming down—with nothing to hold us in the car.

"HELLLP!" Janey and I screamed. "STOP THE RIDE! OUR SAFETY BAR—"

"WHEEEEE!" Everyone else screamed, their hands raised high as the Blister Twister nosedived.

Down . . .

Down . . .

Down . . .

Down . . .

Down . . .

We fell at rocket speed.

THIRTY-TWO

"WHOOOOAH!"

I tried to grab Janey as she flew out of the car into the air.

I missed. And then I went sailing out, too. We were both flying above the coaster cars as they plummeted down.

"YAAAAAAIIIIIIIII!"

Whose scream was that? Was it mine? Was it Janey's?

We flapped our arms wildly like chickens. Why did we think that would help?

We were swooping down now, Janey and I flying together, side by side.

Down . . .

Down . . .

Down . . .

And then we crash-landed.

"OOOOOF!"

That was the sound of me landing in an empty car of the rollercoaster.

THUDDDD!

And that was the sound of Brainy Janey landing beside me.

The car whipped down, then started to roll uphill again. I was panting like a dog, my chest heaving, my breath pumping out in loud wheezes.

Janey's gloves had come off somehow, and she had her hands clamped tightly over her face. Her whole body shuddered and shook. Finally, she lowered her hands and laughed. "What a thrill ride!" she cried.

The roller coaster reached the top and began to roll downhill again.

I gripped the safety bar and shut my eyes.

Everyone screamed as we rocketed down once again.

When I opened my eyes, I saw who was sitting in the car in front of us— Windy Winston and Nat Nerd.

Nat turned his head, his eyes filled with surprise. "I don't remember you being back there," he said.

"We weren't!" I cried.

I was still breathing hard when the cars rolled to a stop. I couldn't wait to climb out. Now I knew why they called it the Blister Twister. I had blisters on my butt from the ups and downs and from landing so hard in the coaster car!

Patty and Peter Perfect went running to Mrs. Hooping-Koff. "We had the *best time!*" Peter exclaimed. "And we didn't even hold on!"

"Peter and I screamed the whole time," Patty said. "We screamed so hard, we lost our voices and started croaking like frogs. We should win ten points—and get extra credit for croaking!"

"*I* should win!" Disgustin' Justin declared. He held up his hands. "Look. I have blisters on my blisters from gripping the safety bar." He shoved his red blisters into Mrs. Hooping-Koff's face.

"Yucko!" she said and backed away. "Put your hands down. That's disgusting."

"You don't win," she said. "And neither do the Perfects. The winners are Adam and Janey."

Mrs. Hooping-Koff waved to us. "Adam and Janey flew from car to car and landed perfectly."

I turned to Janey. "Wow. She saw all of that?"

"They rode in *two* cars—not just one," Mrs. Hooping-Koff said. "So I'm awarding them ten points *each!*"

Janey and I leaped into the air and high-fived. "Yaaaay."

But then Janey turned to Mrs. Hooping-Koff. "Don't we get extra credit for almost dying?"

Our teacher shook her head. "There's no points for almost dying," she said. "You get fifty points for dying, but you're still alive. *Almost* dying doesn't count. Sorry."

"So what's the score?" I asked.

Mrs. Hooping-Koff checked her notepad. "Well . . . let's see. The Perfects have *eighty points*, and Adam and Janey have *ten points*."

I slapped Janey another high five. "We're catching up!" I said.

THIRTY-THREE

Babbling Brooke here, continuing the story.

    I was having so much fun at the park, I wanted to jump up and lead everyone in a cheer. So I did:

  "GO, PARK! GO, PARK! GO, PARK!

  "YOU'RE FUN IN DAY OR DARK!

  "THE RIDES ARE ALL A THRILL!

  "TOO BAD LUKE PUKE GOT ILL!

  "YAAAAAY!"

    I did a double somersault and landed on my back. When I was able to stand again, I realized all my friends had moved on. I'm not sure they had even heard my awesome cheer.

    But that's okay. I was having an amazing time. I only hoped we could win more points. I knew we could do it—if I worked hard to cheer everyone on.

    The park was crowded, and it took me a while to find

my friends. When I found them, they were piling into open cars at the Safari Thrill Ride. So I took off running and jumped into the car next to Wacky Jackie.

"This is supposed to be a cool ride," she said. "It takes you through a swamp and a forest. And you can see hundreds of real animals living in the wild."

The driver was a young man wearing a blue admiral's cap. He stood up and came walking back through the car. "Remember, keep your hands inside the car at all times," he said. "Don't try to pet any animals. These are wild animals, and they will bite."

Nervous Rex started to shake. "What happens if my hand gets b-bitten off?" he asked.

"No problem. We'll refund your money," the driver said.

"B-but I didn't pay any money," Rex said. "I won a contest."

The young man rubbed his chin. "In that case, we'll replace your hand with a plastic one from the gift shop," he said. "So, no worries."

"No worries," Nervous Rex repeated. But he didn't seem all that convinced.

The driver started toward the front of the car. But then he stopped and turned back. "I do have one other announcement to make," he said. "I'm afraid you will not be seeing our hippopotamus today. Our hippo escaped a few weeks ago, and we are still searching for him."

An escaped hippo?

We all turned to Rob Slob. He had a big bag of salted penguin treats in his lap, and his cheeks were covered in dark fish flakes. He raised his hand to ask the driver a question.

"Is the hippo's name Rob Slob Junior?"

The young man blinked. "No, his name is Buttercup."

"Oh, different hippo," Rob said.

Nasty Nancy pointed at Rob. "I thought you were a hippo when I first met you!" she cried.

"People make that mistake all the time," Rob said.

"That's fat-shaming, Nancy," Windy Winston told her. "You're not supposed to do that."

"And what are you?" she snapped back. "You're just a shame!"

"Why do we always h-have to argue?" Nervous Rex asked.

The driver kept his eye on Rob Slob the whole time. "Have you seen a hippo anywhere?" he asked.

Rob thought about it. "No, not really," he said.

Rob is a good liar. No one can read his expression because of all the snack food stuck to his face.

The driver squinted at Rob a while longer. Then he turned to the front and slid behind the wheel.

"Buckle up, everyone," he shouted. "It's going to be an exciting ride!

Unfortunately, we didn't know just how exciting it would turn out to be.

THIRTY-FOUR

The car rolled along under some tall, leafy trees. The dirt path was rough, and we bumped up and down in the narrow car.

Wacky Jackie sat next to me on the outside. As we dipped under some dark shadows, she said, "I hope we see some kitties. I just love kitties. I could never have one because my parents were allergic."

"They were allergic to cats?" I said.

Jackie shook her head. "No, they were allergic to me."

I squinted at her. "Did you forget? The ten of us live in a house without parents. None of us remembers how we even got there. And we don't remember our parents."

"I know," Jackie said. "I just made it up."

"Do you lie like that all the time?" I asked.

"It's not a lie," she said. "It's a joke. You know, like your cheers." Then she smiled and poked me.

"I don't think you'll see any cats," I told her. "Cats don't live in the wild."

"Haven't you ever heard of wildcats?" Brainy Janey chimed in from the seat behind us. "Wildcats are members of the thingamabob species, and they all live in the wild."

"I can't wait to see a thingamabob!" Jackie exclaimed.

"If you'll look to the right, you'll see our two lion cubs, Teddy and Freddy," the driver announced.

And there they were. Wrestling in a patch of tall grass.

"What do lions eat?" Brett Sweat called to the driver.

"Anything they want!" he replied.

"Up ahead is the watering hole where our hippopotamus used to live," he announced, looking back at Rob.

Jackie and I leaned out and saw the big empty mudhole.

"We're pretty sure we'll find the hippo soon," the driver said. "It's really hard for him to blend into a crowd."

I fought back the urge to shout out the truth—that the missing hippo was in our living room right this minute. But it was Rob Slob's hippo, and it was up to him to tell the driver where he was.

I turned and saw Rob Slob lean toward the driver. "How can we identify your hippo?" he asked.

"Well . . . he looks like a hippo," the driver replied. "That will probably help you narrow it down."

"Can you describe him?"

"Yes, I can. He's as big as a hippo and closely resembles a hippo."

"I'm starting to get it," Rob said, nodding.

"Why are you asking all these questions?" the driver asked.

"No reason," Rob said. "Because I haven't seen your hippo, and he isn't in our house acting as our new housekeeper."

"Well, if you ever see him," the driver called, "give us a shout, okay?"

The car turned into flat grasslands. We saw ostriches standing on a low hill. Swans were swimming in a small, oval-shaped pond. A cluster of pink flamingos stood on the side.

"Beyond those trees, the land changes again," the driver said. "We find ourselves on the dry plains. And over there . . . one of our treasures . . . a white rhinoceros."

"Whoa. Check that out!" I cried.

And then everyone gasped in shock as Rob Slob

jumped to his feet. For some reason, Rob leaped out of
the car. He hit the ground hard, bounced a few times—
and then took off, running toward the rhinoceros.

THIRTY-FIVE

The enormous rhinoceros raised its head and watched as Rob Slob came running toward it. With everyone screaming in horror, the car came to a screeching stop.

Our driver jumped to his feet and watched wide-eyed as Rob raced toward the huge creature. "What is he doing?" he cried, clapping his hands to the side of his face. "What is he *doing*? He could get hurt. And I could get *fired* for this!"

"I think I know," Wacky Jackie said. "He told me he always wanted to ride a white rhinoceros."

"Huh?" the driver's mouth dropped open to his knees. "He—*what*?!"

Jackie nodded. "He told me it was on his bucket list. Rob said he always had this dream of riding a white rhino."

"But—but—" the driver stammered. "*No one* rides a rhinoceros!"

"Tell that to Rob," Jackie said.

We all screamed again as Rob Slob ran up to the giant rhino—and leaped onto its back.

It took a few seconds for Rob to get his balance. Then he sat up straight with his legs over the animal's sides and raised his fists high above his head in triumph.

Rob shouted something, but I couldn't hear it over everyone's screams and cries. I was so scared, I squeezed Wacky Jackie's hand tightly. My heart was racing in my chest like a frightened rabbit.

Rob waved his arm high, celebrating his victory. As Rob cheered himself, the rhino began to move. It took a few steps, then picked up speed.

Then it lowered its head, and Rob began to slide forward.

The rhino lowered its head a little more. And then it flipped Rob into the air.

Rob's mouth opened wide and he screamed as he came down hard—on the rhino's horn.

Our screams were so loud, I covered my ears and shut my eyes tight.

This can't be happening, I told myself. *This is supposed to be an amusement park. But this wasn't amusing at all!*

When I opened my eyes, Rob Slob was back in the car, grinning. "That was *awesome!*" he exclaimed.

Adam Bomb grabbed him by the shoulder. "Rob, you just landed on a rhinoceros horn," he said. "How can you be okay?"

"It's the salt," Rob explained, pulling up his shirt. "See? I have a hard, two-inch layer of salt on my chest. It's from the tortilla chips I eat. There's no way that rhino horn could get through my layer of salt."

"Wow, it pays to be a slob," I said.

"Maybe if we all ate like Rob, we could become superheroes," Wacky Jackie said. "Or safari daredevils."

"Ten points for Rob Slob," Mrs. Hooping-Koff announced.

Patty Perfect fainted, but only after her brother Peter—and our driver—also passed out!

THIRTY-SIX

As I was saying in Chapter Thirty, why do people think I talk too much? I'm Windy Winston, and I would like to continue the story.

I love continuing stories. Because if you don't continue them, you can't get to the end. You know what I mean?

Let's say you start a story. And you are really interested in hearing how the story ends. But the person telling the story just yaks and yaks and yaks, and goes off on one tangent after another. But all you want to do is find out the ending of the story.

But you can't even find out what happens next because he keeps talking. And talking.

I hate when that happens, don't you?

Here's my question: Is it more fun to *tell* a story or to *listen* to a story?

I don't really know the answer to that one.

The one thing I *did* know was that those two Perfect twins were winning the contest. We were all having a good time at Six Thrills. But they were having the *best* time. And that teacher, Mrs. Hoof-and-Mouth-Disease (I think that's her name), was awarding them all the points.

Then that kid Rob Slob jumped on top of a rhinoceros, and he scored points for that.

I said to my friend Disgustin' Justin, "Maybe we should jump on top of something dangerous. Then we could score points, too."

"Worth a try," Justin replied.

But none of my other friends agreed with us, so we didn't try it.

"One time, I jumped off a kangaroo," Nat Nerd told me.

I stared at him. "You did? How could you do that?"

"Well . . . it was in a dream," he said. "But it seemed very real."

We followed the other kids to our next activity, where a big red sign over the entrance read:

BALLS OF DOOM

We stepped into the arena—a large circle filled with enormous rubber balls that were all different colors.

As I walked closer, I saw that the balls had handles. Kids sat on the balls and gripped the handles with both hands, then bounced all over the arena floor.

They bounced high, and bounced into one another, bouncing in all directions. It looked like a lot of fun, especially if you like bouncing.

"Let's see who will win points for having the best time bouncing," said Mrs. Hoop-De-Doo, or whatever her name was.

"Peter and I will *definitely* win this one!" Patty Perfect exclaimed. "We are great at bouncing. It's one of our hobbies."

"We bounce all the time," Peter added. "Sometimes we bounce for hours at home. We're perfect bouncers."

"Your friend Junkfood John can bounce without a ball!" Nasty Nancy said.

Babbling Brooke stepped up to her. "Hey, that's fat-shaming!" she scolded. "Don't make fun of John because he's obese!"

"What else should we make fun of him about?" Nancy snapped back.

Junkfood John held up a large bag. "Would anyone like to share these Guppy Crisps? They're fishy *and* crunchy."

"Sure," Disgustin' Justin said, grabbing a handful from the bag and shoving them into his mouth. He chewed for a few seconds, then his eyes bulged and he spat the whole mouthful all over the ground.

"You have to watch out for the guppy eyeballs," Junkfood John warned. But it was too late.

"Okay, everyone," the teacher announced. "Jump on a ball and let's see some great bouncing."

So we all ran into the arena and climbed onto the Balls of Doom and started to bounce.

And that's when something seriously strange happened.

THIRTY-SEVEN

Junkfood John here. I'll continue the story because Windy Winston talks too much and we may never get to the end of the story. When he starts talking, I want to tear my ears off and stuff them in my pockets.

But that might hurt.

I've never seen a guy talk so much. He was even talking to himself as he bounced across the floor on a big yellow ball.

I hoisted myself onto a purple ball and grabbed the handle with one hand. It's hard to bounce and hold a bag of Guppy Crisps at the same time. I slipped off the ball twice and nearly lost some of my guppy treats.

I also had a bag of nacho cheese gummy worms in my back pocket. That was my mid-mid-mid-morning

snack. I had to be careful, because I didn't want to crush the bag as I bounced.

I leaned forward and started to bounce higher.

"WHOOOOAAH!" I bounced right into Cranky Frankie and sent him bouncing against the wall. He shouted something, and I was glad I couldn't hear what he said.

Then someone bounced from behind and sent me sailing over the floor.

This was fun. We were all screaming and laughing ... bouncing high . . . crashing into one another. Then I glimpsed the Perfect twins. They were sitting on matching pink balls and bouncing in unison, side by side.

Wacky Jackie then bounced into Brett Sweat, and they both bumped into Nat Nerd, who bumped into Handy Sandy, and they all bounced against the arena wall.

And then something weird happened. I don't want to believe it, but I saw it with my own eyes. So I *have* to believe it.

Wacky Jackie scrunched down on her green ball and then shot her legs up hard.

Her ball lifted off the floor and she zoomed like a rocket, straight at the ceiling.

Jackie bounced higher than anyone else.

And then—she *disappeared.*

I watched her. I'm not joking. She just . . . vanished.

I dragged my shoes on the floor to stop bouncing. A few other kids stopped bouncing, too, and climbed off their balls. And soon we were all standing there, confused.

Mrs. Hooping-Koff gazed all around and asked, "Where is Wacky Jackie? Where did she go?"

No one could answer.

But finally, Brainy Janey stepped forward. "I know where Jackie went," she said.

We all turned to listen to her. The only sound was me crunching Guppy Crisps as I finished the bag.

"I know where Jackie went," Brainy Janey repeated. "She bounced so high, *she bounced into the next book.*"

"Huh?" I gasped. "Wha—?"

"Jackie bounced into the next book in this series," Janey explained. "She bounced into Garbage Pail Kids: Book Three, *Camp Daze.* I'm afraid you won't see Jackie again until you read that book."

"Well, that explains it," Mrs. Hooping-Koff said. "If Jackie was still here, I'd award her ten points. So I guess I'll just give *minus-ten* to everyone else. Does that make sense?"

THIRTY-EIGHT

Wacky Jackie here.

I'm in the next book in this series, and I don't see anyone else.

I seem to be the only one in this place.

I'm so *confused*—I'm on a mostly blank page.

How long will I have to wait for the others to catch up?

I finally get a chance to tell part of our story, and *this* is what R.L. Stine does to me?

THIRTY-NINE

Nervous Rex here again. I guess *I'll* tell you what happened next.

After Wacky Jackie disappeared, most of us kids went on a roller coaster called the Haircut.

I stayed back because roller coasters make me nervous. Anything that moves fast makes me nervous. I mean, why does a roller coaster have to be fast, anyway?

I asked Adam Bomb, "Why is this one called the Haircut?"

He said, "Because it goes so fast, it has 5G wind force, and it blows off all your hair. But they give you these hair caps, which will protect your head."

"Th-that sounds like fun," I replied. Of course, I was being sarcastic. I wouldn't go anywhere near that coaster. Besides, look at me: I don't really need a haircut.

And haircuts always make me nervous, too. I mean,

what if they miss with the scissors and cut off an ear? Do you still have to pay if that happens?

Luke Puke didn't go on the coaster, either. He said 5G wind forces always make him puke. He said 4G is one thing, but 5G was just too much.

Junkfood John found a food booth that sold frog knuckles on a stick. That's his favorite before-lunch snack, so he also stayed off the coaster and enjoyed his frog knuckles.

"We have a 5G wind force room at home," Peter Perfect bragged. "Patty and I use it to blow dry our hair in the morning."

"5G's good for our skin, too," Patty said. "That's why we always have a perfect, rosy glow."

"We are going to have the *best* time on this roller coaster," Peter added.

I watched as everyone hurried into the line for the Haircut. Then I waited by the exit for them to come out. I could hear the coaster cars rumbling and roaring and squealing with incredible speed. And I could hear a lot of people screaming their heads off.

All that screaming made me nervous. Doesn't it make *you* nervous, too, when you hear a lot of people screaming in terror?

I hugged myself tightly as I stood by the exit and waited for everyone to come out. After about ten minutes, my friends and the others came staggering out. They were shaking their heads and laughing. But it wasn't *ha-ha* laughter. It was the kind of laughter that says, *Wow, I'm so happy to still be alive.*

They were all sucking in big mouthfuls of air and mopping sweat off their foreheads. "That was awesome!" Peter Perfect cried. But his voice was tiny and shaky when he said it.

The kids all remembered to wear their hair caps, so they looked okay. But it took me a while to recognize Mrs. Hooping-Koff—because she was totally bald!

Her head looked like a shiny pink egg.

She staggered closer, and I realized that her eyes were no longer on the front of her head. They had been blown to the back!

It took us a while to help her tug them into place. Then her whole body shuddered and shook, like a dog after a bath. She reached into her pocketbook and pulled out a hairbrush.

I don't think she knew she was bald! But no one was brave enough to tell her. Not even Principal Grunt.

"Okay, people," she shouted. "I think we are done. That ends our day at Six Thrills. I hope you all had a wonderful time!"

"Who won the contest?" Patty Perfect asked. "Tell us—who won?"

"Well . . . let me see," our teacher replied. She started to dig in her pocketbook. "I have the list right here. The winner is . . ."

FORTY

Mrs. Hooping-Koff looked around in her pocket-book. It made me nervous to watch her. I hate it when people paw around in their bags. What if there's something in there and it bites you?

Do you ever think of *that*?

Well, I do.

I guess that's why they call me Nervous Rex.

Our teacher was looking for her notepad where she kept the score, but she couldn't find it.

"Hmmmm," she muttered, opening her purse wide and searching frantically.

"Who won?" Nat Nerd cried. "Can we say it was a tie just so we can all stop fighting?"

"Who won?" Brainy Janey asked. "Was it close? I can help you do the math. I'm good with numbers."

Miss Hooping-Koff sighed and lowered her

pocketbook to the ground. "Wouldn't you know it?" she murmured. "I lost my notepad."

Everyone gasped.

Our teacher wrinkled up her bald head. "I think the 5G blew it away."

"So . . . we don't have a winner?" Nasty Nancy demanded.

Mrs. Hooping-Koff nodded. "Oh, sure we do. The Perfect twins win. You know . . . they *always* win."

"YAAAAAAY!" Patty and Peter Perfect jumped up and down and high fived, celebrating their victory.

"What do we win?" Patty asked breathlessly when she and her brother finally settled down.

"Yes. What is our prize, teacher?" Peter Perfect asked.

Mrs. Hooping-Koff smiled at them. "The prize is a ride home in my car. I'm afraid the bus left an hour ago. The rest of you will just have to walk."

FORTY-ONE

" Walk home?" I don't believe it!" Adam Bomb cried.

And just like that he exploded all over everyone. So not only did we have to walk home, but we had to carry his pieces home with us, too.

It was a *long* walk back to Smellville, so I could understand why Adam took the news so hard. It always makes me nervous when he explodes and goes flying everywhere.

But he always pulls himself back together eventually.

We all agreed we had an awesome time at the Six Thrills Amusement Park. But it wasn't worth the walk home.

We headed out in single file along the highway with the five newcomers—the kids who also claim to be the Garbage Pail Kids. Brett Sweat had to stop and mop his forehead every few minutes. Windy Winston kept talking—to himself. Disgustin' Justin practiced *lonnnng,* loud burps as he walked. Nat Nerd kept reminding him to mind his manners. And Nasty Nancy kept making nasty comments about all of us the whole way home.

But everything went okay until we reached Smellville.

The other kids said they live in Smellville North, and we live in Smellville South. So we had to split up and say goodbye.

"Maybe we can have a playdate sometime," Windy Winston said. "You could come visit us and see how the *real* Garbage Pail Kids live!"

"*We're* the real Garbage Pail Kids!" Cranky Frankie shouted.

"No—we are!"

"No way—we are!"

And before you knew it, we were all punching one another and scratching and elbowing and kneeing and wrestling in the dirt on the side of the road. It was a horrible fight, and it didn't end until Nat Nerd shouted: "Manners, everyone! Manners!"

And with that, we all turned and stomped away in our separate directions.

I couldn't *wait* to get home.

"I just want to hang out in the living room and chill," Handy Sandy said.

"I'm going to sink into the couch, eat some chips, and binge as many episodes of *Jonny Pantsfalldown* as I can," Junkfood John said.

Rob Slob agreed. "That sounds like heaven."

It was night when our house came into view. It's not a great house, but it was ours. Home sweet home.

Only it wasn't.

When we stepped into the front door—we let out cries of horror.

Rob Slob Junior stood with a couch leg poking out of his mouth. The room was clean. And bare. *Very bare.*

Our housekeeper ate the living room.

We stood there gaping in silence. No one said a word.

Finally, Rob Slob spoke up. "Think we should return him? Or should we give him a second chance?"

R.L. STINE has more than 400 million English-language books in print, plus international editions in thirty-two languages, making him one of the most popular children's authors of all time. Besides Goosebumps, he has written series including Fear Street, Rotten School, Mostly Ghostly, the Nightmare Room, Dangerous Girls, and Just Beyond. Stine lives in New York City with his wife, Jane, an editor and publisher.

JEFF ZAPATA has worked on comic books and trading cards for more than twenty-five years, including thirteen gross, memorable ones as an editor, art director, and artist on Garbage Pail Kids and other brands at the Topps Company.

FRED WHEATON has been wallowing in the Garbage Pail at Topps since 2006, contributing disgusting concepts, final art, comics, and sketch cards. He lives in Washington, DC, with his wife and their three kids.

JOE SIMKO is an artist known for his happy-horror style. He is one of the premiere Garbage Pail Kids illustrators for the Topps Company and lives in New York City with his wife, son, dog, and many, many boxes of cereal.

THE TOPPS COMPANY, INC., originator of Garbage Pail Kids, Mars Attacks, and Bazooka Joe brands, was founded in 1938 and is the preeminent creator and marketer of physical and digital trading cards, entertainment products, and distinctive confectionery.